NEVER CON A CON MAN

An Arizona High Country Mystery

BY

SUZANNE FLOYD

COPYRIGHT

This is a work of fiction. All characters in this book have no existence outside the imagination of the author. The town of Pine Mountain is a composite of many small towns anywhere.

Copyright November 2017 by Suzanne Floyd. All rights reserved. No part of this book may be reproduced in any form, save for inclusion of brief quotations in a review, without the written permission of the author. www.SuzanneFloyd.com

Cover by Bella Media Management

    I dedicate this book to my husband Paul and our daughters, Camala and Shannon, and all my family. Thanks for all your support and encouragement.

    "Once Lost, now found. Eternally thankful!" Our Daily Bread

CHAPTER ONE

Hiding in the shadows of the auditorium, Max watched his big brother give the town the bad news. It wasn't going very well. Everyone knows I'm a screw-up, he thought, so it's easy for people to assume I'm also a thief. But I'm not. Disappearing made it look bad, but he didn't have a choice.

What had started out as a game, turned real and nasty when he discovered the money was missing for real from the town's accounts. Confronting his gaming partner was when it turned nasty. It was either run, or die. He was prepared to die if necessary. He'd made his peace with God. But he didn't want to die with Jim believing he had betrayed him again. He had the evidence to prove he was innocent, but who would believe him?

Scanning the many faces in the crowded room, his gaze settled on the one person who would give him the benefit of a doubt before jumping to conclusions. At least he hoped she would. Getting the proof to her might be a problem though. He had to find a way before he was caught, either by the police or the embezzler. It would be better to be caught by the police. His nephew was now the Chief of Police. But would he listen to my story?

His ribs ached from the pummeling he'd sustained at the hands of a man he'd thought of as his friend. Now he knew better. He had everyone fooled with his mild manners and refined talk. When things didn't go his way, or when he was cornered, he was just as evil as everyone else. He hadn't realized his lover was playing him for a fool. He gave his head a shake. How he'd let her con him that way. Well, two could play that game. He'd been a con man most of his life, now he'd see who was the better con artist.

His thoughts were wandering, he needed to concentrate, or things would get even worse. Slipping away into the dark, he hoped he could see the only person who could help him before it was too late.

~~~

"The town coffers are tapped out." Mayor Jim Cox stood on the stage of the big auditorium. His statement was met with stunned silence. Pandemonium broke out with the next statement. "We're going to have to raise taxes." I cringed at both of those announcements. There must have been a better way of putting that. But my former step-father wasn't always the most diplomatic guy.

"How did that happen?" "You can't do that." "Where did the money go?" Everyone was talking at once.

Standing behind the table at the front of the room, Jim looked all official. His white hair was perfectly groomed, his shirt starched so stiff I was surprised he could move. As mayor of the small town of Pine Mountain, it was his duty to report to the citizens what was happening. It was also his duty to make sure the town was run properly. Right now, neither of those things was going very well for him.

"Settle down, folks." He pounded the gavel on the table without any result. Finally a shrill whistle brought the silence he had been hoping for.

"How did this happen?" With order finally restored, people were taking turns asking questions. I couldn't see who asked the question. The meeting was being held in the high school auditorium in order to fit everyone in. The room was packed to capacity.

From my vantage point at the side of the room, I surveyed the crowd. It wasn't just citizens of Pine Mountain attending the meeting. People who lived outside the town boundaries were in attendance as well. This would affect everyone, not simply those living within the town limits. Jim had been pushing to annex some of the outer areas. This wasn't going to help his cause.

"The matter is being investigated," Jim stated. Beads of sweat glistened on his forehead. The tight control he held on his temper was beginning to slip. As much as he enjoyed his position as mayor, he didn't like being in the hot seat. "Until we can get it sorted out, we need to have funds to run the town."

I felt sorry for him. He truly loved this town, and wanted to do what was best. Of course, some people would say I'm slightly prejudiced since he is one of my step-fathers. Former step-father, that is.

"Who took the money?" Several people nodded their heads at the question.

"I'm not really sure. As I said, this is an ongoing investigation."

"Where's Max? Maybe he can explain what happened to the money," Dennis Baxter stood up to ask his question. Dennis and his wife Darlene owned *DD's Diner,* the small café in town. "As town treasurer, shouldn't he be here tonight?"

"Um, well, that's another thing. I don't know where Max is right now." Jim swiped at the sweat that had started running down his face. His starched shirt was beginning to wilt. Max is Jim's younger brother, and a screw-up. Jim had been covering for him for as long as I'd known them. My heart broke for him now.

There were more shouted questions from all corners of the room. After another shrill whistle, people began to settle down. Jill Davidson's whistle worked better than pounding the gavel on the table. Jill and her twin sister had been my best friends when I lived here before. I'd always wanted to whistle like that, but you can't teach someone to whistle.

"I promise we'll get to the bottom of this," Jim said. "Until that happens though, we need to get some funds in the town treasury."

"You can't increase taxes without a special election." Bud Walker spoke up this time. The roots of most of those present went as deep as Jim's. No one wanted more taxes, but they didn't want the town to default either. I wasn't sure how Jim and the town council were going to handle this.

"How do you expect the town services to continue without funds to pay for them?" Jim asked. He was getting agitated.

"As it stands right now, some of the nonessential town services will have to be cut."

I released a pent up sigh. *Nonessential services like the library.* As the recently hired head librarian, that meant I might be out of a job in the very near future. *Darn you, Max.* I was selfishly thinking only of myself. This went a lot farther than my little corner of the world.

"We're open to any suggestions," Jim said, bringing my thoughts back to the room. So far, the other four members of the town council hadn't said a word. People grumbled, but no one had a good solution to the problem.

"Find Max and you'll find the money. If he hasn't gambled it away, that is." I looked around trying to see who was speaking. I didn't recognize the voice. "Everybody knew you shouldn't have given him the job of handling the town's money. He never could keep his hands off of what wasn't his." Jim's face was crimson with the tight control he had on his temper now.

"Until the investigation is finished, you can't pin this on Max," Jim snapped. "We don't know what happened. If you don't have anything constructive to add, Wally, keep your mouth shut."

Of course it would be Wally Miller, I thought. There had been bad blood between Wally and Max going as far back as high school. He certainly knew how to carry a grudge. It wouldn't matter to him if this hurt Jim and the rest of the family.

Nothing had been resolved by the time the meeting was adjourned. The treasury was still empty, and no one was willing or could afford to pay more taxes. As a relative newcomer and an outsider to boot, it wasn't my place to pass judgment, or make suggestions.

As Wally headed to the door, he glared at me. I assumed he had been opposed to Jim hiring me as well. Wally didn't like anything or anyone related to the Cox family. I guess that included me. "Find Max and you'll find our money," he growled. Did he mean I should find Max?

~~~

"I screwed up. I underestimated him. How did I get roped into this?" He knew exactly how it had happened. He never was a good judge of character. This time his lack of good judgment could land him in prison, or worse.

His thoughts were spinning out of control, and he felt sick to his stomach. He'd let his good sense be overruled by the need for fast cash. He tried to tell himself he was doing this for their future, but that wasn't the complete truth. He'd let himself be conned into believing no one would catch on to what they were doing. Now he was in a real jam. He shook his head. She could talk the devil out of hell, she was that good.

He thought he'd covered his tracks, but what if he hadn't? What if Max was better than she was? What if he was caught? He didn't want go to jail. She wouldn't come to his rescue that was for sure.

He drew a deep breath, letting it out slowly. *I have to remain calm,* he told himself. *I need to maintain the perception of innocence.* He slipped out the side door as soon as the meeting broke up. He couldn't pretend to be calm any longer.

~~~

Waiting until everyone had left, I slowly made my way over to Jim. "Um, Jim, is there anything I can do to help?" I stepped up to the table where he sat with his head in his hands.

"Well, hi there, kiddo. Thanks for coming tonight. Sorry it was such a downer." He tried to put on a happy face.

"Do you know where Max is? What really happened to the money?"

His broad shoulders slumped. "I can't answer either of those questions. I wish I could. I don't want to believe my little brother would embezzle the town funds, but what else am I supposed to think? He's gone, and so is the money. If I find out he did this, I'll shoot him myself."

It was a typical Jim reaction. His temper flashed in an

instant, but it never lasted more than a few seconds. He slumped back against the chair, his temper already fizzled out.

I knew he didn't mean what he said. If it turned out that Max had embezzled the funds, Jim would do whatever he could to help him out of the mess, even if it meant replacing the money out of his own pocket. That meant he would have to hock everything he owned, including the hardware store and ranch that had been in his family for four generations. He hadn't said how much money was missing, but I assumed it was a great deal.

"The worst part is Wally," he added softly. "He'll never let me forget this stain on our family name if it turns out Max is to blame."

"I'm sorry, Jim." I didn't know what else to say.

He drew a deep breath, letting it out slowly. I'd only been back in Pine Mountain for six months, but the small town meant a lot to me. It was the one place I'd lived the longest while growing up.

My mom had married Jim when I was ten. The five years we lived here held many happy memories for me. It was the longest stretch I'd lived in one spot until I graduated from high school. Because my half-brother Tim was Jim's son, I had kept in contact with him.

"What are you going to do? How are you going to be able to pay the town's bills?"

"You don't have to worry about it, Holly. I'll figure something out." Again his shoulders slumped, and his face got red. "I guess you do have to worry about it. If we can't afford to pay our bills that means we can't pay salaries either." He huffed out a breath. "I'll make sure you get paid, even if I pay you myself."

"No, Jim. I don't want you to do that." He started to argue, but I held up my hand. "It wouldn't be fair to the other employees who lose their jobs if I get to keep mine. I have a nice nest egg saved up. I'll get by until you get this figured out."

He stood up, giving me a warm hug. "I always wished you were my daughter, not just my step-daughter. I'm glad you moved back home." He gave another sigh as he sank back into his chair. "We'll get this thing figured out," he assured me again. "Until then, the town will get by. I'm afraid I didn't handle things very well tonight. I just wish Max hadn't disappeared at the same time the money did. It makes him look guilty even if he isn't."

Max is ten years younger than Jim. When I first lived in Pine Mountain, he came and went like the wind. The last time he came back, it appeared that he had turned his life around. That's when Jim gave him the job as town treasurer. Now he felt responsible for the missing money. If Max took the money, I suppose he was.

"Hey, how's your mom doing?" I accepted the subject change. "I heard she got married again." I wasn't surprised that he knew about that. Tim would have kept him informed. "Last time I talked to Tim, they were getting ready to move, but he didn't say where."

"Mom's fine," I said. "They're living in Florida for now. Tim's pretty excited about that. He loves the beach." At thirteen, Tim was just discovering girls. The fact that they wore bikinis at the beach certainly didn't hurt. "I'm not sure how long they'll be staying there though. I'm sure when the first hurricane hits, Mom will be ready to pull up stakes." I kept hoping she would finally settle down.

"Well, tell them I said hi," Jim said. "Ted sounds like a nice guy. Tim seems to like him." He paused for a minute, releasing a heavy sigh. "That's more than I can say about his feelings for Jane."

Jane is Jim's third wife, and Tim wasn't crazy about her. He'd spent almost a half hour grumbling about her after his last visit with his dad. I couldn't blame him though. She was a little hard to get close to.

"How is Jane? I didn't see her here tonight." In fact I hadn't seen her in town for more than a week.

"She's visiting her mom in Denver with the baby." It surprised me that she took Hannah with her, but I kept that thought to myself. Most of the time, Jane pawned the eleven-month-old-off on anyone willing to babysit. In the six months I'd been in town, I'd spent almost as much time with her as Jane did.

"They should be home next week," he added. "I miss her, them," he quickly corrected. Who did he really miss? My money was on the baby. From my perspective, it didn't look like this marriage was going to last. My heart went out to Hannah. The children of divorce were always the ones to suffer the most.

I'd been surprised when Jim married someone only a few years older than me. It surprised me even more when Jane got pregnant within months of the wedding. She didn't strike me as the motherly type. I had tried to make friends with her, but she hadn't been interested. Unless she needed a babysitter, of course.

Standing up, Jim gathered his papers together. "Thanks again for coming tonight, Holly. I'm glad you decided to move back. I've missed you. I'll do my best to make sure you don't miss any paychecks." Placing a kiss on my cheek, he turned to leave.

My heart went out to him. It couldn't have been easy giving this kind of news to the town. He knew everyone would blame Max, and by extension, they would blame him. The fact that Max was also missing didn't look good.

I pulled my sweater closed when I stepped outside. The wind whipped my reddish-blonde hair into my face. The night air had a bit of a chill to it at this time of year. In the White Mountains of Arizona, fall came earlier than it did in Phoenix where I'd spent the last few years.

"Hi, Holly. How's Dad doing?" Giving a start, I whirled around with my hand over my heart to keep it from jumping out of my chest. I hadn't seen the tall figure leaning against the side of the building.

"Sorry, I didn't mean to scare you." The smile playing around his full lips said just the opposite. Drake had always been a tease, and I had been his favorite target. Two years older than my twenty-four years, Drake is Jim's oldest and one of my many former step-brothers. He pushed away from the wall, stepping up beside me. After a hitch in the Air Force, he'd settled in Pine Mountain. He was the police chief now.

During my early teens, Drake had been my first crush. Even without any blood ties between us, it always felt a little creepy to let it go any farther than a crush.

"I didn't see you inside. Why didn't you come in? I thought you'd want to be there for your dad." I frowned up at him. At five feet ten, he was several inches taller than my five foot three, so that I had to tilt my head back to look at him.

When he shrugged, I tried not to notice how the material of his uniform shirt tightened across his broad shoulders. Apparently my crush hadn't ended when I moved away.

Not what anyone would call conventionally handsome, he had a commanding presence. He filled out the uniform better than most men would. Even when we were in school, he had spent hours working out in the gym. Now the muscles in his arms and chest rippled each time he moved. The bump on his nose spoke of a fight he'd been in as a teenager; a fight he started defending me.

"I was there to make sure things didn't get out of hand." He shook his head. "I thought for a minute I was going to have to pull Dad off of Wally. That guy's a real a...jerk," he finished. "Once talk settled down, I slipped out. Dad's still trying to cover for Uncle Max." He gave a weary sigh. "I don't know why he would disappear like this. It makes him look bad, and doesn't make it easy for the rest of the family living in town."

I frowned at him. "Do you think Max embezzled the money? Why would he do something like that?" I didn't want to believe Max would do that to the town, or his brother.

"Max was a screw-up, no doubt about that, but I thought

he'd changed." He shook his head. A sun-bleached lock of hair fell over his forehead. I tried not to notice that either. "I hate to think he would do something like that, but I just can't say." We started down the auditorium steps.

"Have you talked to the assistant treasurer? He should be the one with the secondary authorization to transfer money."

He bristled at my question. "I don't need you telling me how to do my job."

"I wasn't telling you how to do your job." It was my turn to bristle. "I just asked a simple question." I turned away from him. I wasn't going to stick around if he was going to argue with me.

His long strides kept pace with mine. "To answer your question, I have talked to him. He hadn't been aware there were any problems with the accounts until this morning. When Max failed to show up and didn't call in sick, he started checking. That's when he discovered the accounts were empty."

He drew a deep breath of cool air, and changed the subject. "You getting settled in here all right?"

"Yeah, after all the moving I did in my growing up years, I learned to settle pretty fast." I had spent every summer with Dad in Texas, and the school year with Mom. I just never knew where that would be. That made school a little rough.

"Yeah, it would get tough after a while. I was always glad Mom didn't insist I go with her when she and Dad split up."

"I saw her a few times while I was in college. She hasn't changed much."

He gave a small chuckle. "She still comes up for the holidays. As you can imagine, that doesn't go over very well with this wife."

"No, I imagine it doesn't." Jane wanted to be the center of everyone's attention. She wouldn't want an ex-wife hanging around. During the time I'd lived in Pine Mountain, Mona had joined us for every holiday. There was no need to extend an invitation, she simply showed up. That's just the way things were.

I always thought she might have been part of the reason Jim and Mom split up. But that wasn't the case. Mom has a touch of wanderlust, as well as a short attention span. She never wanted to settle in one place for very long.

Using the key fob, I unlocked the door of my car. Drake opened the door for me, holding it open until I got in. "It's good to have you back in town, Holly. See you around." He watched while I pulled out of the lot.

I gave a sigh. "Too bad he's one of my steps," I told myself. "He's one good-looking man." Pushing that thought aside, my thoughts returned to the missing money. Had Max embezzled the funds? Why would he do something like that? He had to know people would blame Jim for hiring him.

The little house I was renting sat at the edge of town, and backed up to the national forest. Pulling into the drive, I realized I forgot to turn on the outside light before leaving for the meeting. Once the sun dropped over the mountain, it got dark fast. There were no street lights out here.

My heart skipped a beat when the shadows shifted around the side of the house. Had the wind stirred the trees behind the house? Or was someone hiding out in the forest waiting for me to get out of my car? City life instilled caution in me that most people living here didn't have. I made sure my doors were locked, even when I was home.

I waited for several beats before opening the car door. When nothing else moved, I gathered my courage, making a run for the back door. Once inside, I made sure all the doors and windows were securely locked. Growing up, I was never alone no matter where I lived. Even in college, I'd had roommates. Being alone was a little unnerving now. Silence isn't always golden.

I let out a startled squeal when someone knocked on the back door. Someone had been out there. Would they try to break in? "Holly, it's Bill. Are you all right?" His muffled voice came through the door.

The breath I'd been holding escaped in a whoosh. I sagged against the counter for a minute before unlocking the door. Bill is Jim's son, and Drake's only full brother. He came around every now and then to check up on me. I hadn't seen him for a couple of weeks though.

"Were you out in the woods watching for me to come home?" I questioned before stepping back to let him in the house.

"No. I just got here. I walked over from my place. Why did you scream?" A frown drew his eyebrows together over his dark eyes. There was only a slight resemblance between him and Drake. He looked more like his mother than Jim.

"You scared me," I accused. "It's after nine o'clock. I wasn't expecting any visitors. Did you see anyone out there?"

"What's going on, Holly? Why are you so spooked?"

I flopped down on the couch, resting my head against the back cushion. "Everything was dark when I came home. I thought I saw something move outside."

"I didn't see anything, but I wasn't looking for the boogeyman either." He gave a chuckle. "I came over to find out how things went for Dad at the meeting? I couldn't make it." Dismissing my fear, he sat down across from me. Bill is a few months younger than me, and I had teased him that I was his big sister. Like several other of my steps, we had remained friends after I moved away. I always thought he had a crush on me, like I'd had on Drake. Nothing would ever come of it for either of us.

"I feel bad for him," I said on a sigh. "People are going to blame him if it turns out Max took the money."

He nodded his head. "I know, but I don't think Uncle Max would do something like that. Since he came back to town, he's changed. I think he even has a girlfriend."

"Do you know who she is?" When he shook his head, I continued. "Can you think of anyone who would do this?" He knew the people in town better than I did even though he spent most of his time away from town with the Forest Service.

"If Wally Miller thought it would get Dad or Max in trouble, I can see him doing just about anything," he said, giving his dark head a shake. "I don't know how he could do it though. He doesn't have anything to do with town business. I don't know anyone else who would try to hurt Dad or the town." He left a few minutes later, disappearing into the dark night. He knew the trails through the forest like the back of his hand, and didn't worry about wild animals.

Okay, so Wally had no way to access the town's accounts that left him out. Who besides Max had access? I tried to think, but I was too tired.

I had just crawled into bed when the phone rang. It was too late for a social call. This could only be bad news.

~~~

"Are we really going to get away with this?" He wrung his hands worriedly. *They were sitting in the living room at his small apartment. He hated everything about the apartment and the town. He couldn't wait to get out of there* *"Are you sure Max wasn't able to stop us?"*

"Of course I'm sure. I don't leave things to chance. He's going to find out I'm smarter than he is. Everything points to him. Disappearing makes him look guilty. We just need to act as shocked as everyone else. As long as he's on the run, they'll blame him. Everyone knows he's a screw-up."

"Aren't you afraid he'll tell his brother or nephew?"

"Trust me. I know what I'm doing. Just play your part, and no one will ever find out."

CHAPTER TWO

"Are you alone, Holly?" The hushed, raspy voice sent chills down my spine. This sounded more like an obscene phone call than an emergency.

"Who is this?" I snapped, angry at the thought that someone would call me to talk dirty.

"It's Max. If someone is with you, please don't say my name."

"Max? Where are you? Why are you calling me?"

"Are you alone?" he asked again, urgency rang through his voice. "Is Bill still there?"

"What? No, he left a long time ago. It's after eleven o'clock. "What's going on? How did you know Bill was here?" My stomach was churning. Had he been outside my house when I came home? Was it his shadow I'd seen moving outside?

I hadn't been very close to him when I lived in Pine Mountain as a child. Since moving back six months ago, I'd gotten to know him a little better. But we still weren't close. I didn't understand why he would be calling me. "Why did you disappear?"

"I don't have much time to talk, so you need to listen to me and not ask questions. I didn't do what they're saying, but not many people are going to believe that. Tell Jim I'm sorry. I know what it looks like, but someone is framing me. I didn't take the money. I would never do that. You have to believe me, I didn't do it." The words came out in a rush.

"Come back to town so Drake can prove that. Running away only makes you look guilty."

"NO, no," he repeated softer. He was still talking in a whisper. "I can't come back yet. Tell Jim it wasn't me. Tell Drake to keep looking. You worked at a bank when you were in college. Maybe you could help Drake. Tell them I'm sorry." Before I could say anything further, the line went dead. I didn't know what to think. Why had he called me? Why not call Drake or Jim? What gave him the idea that I could help the police? I didn't know what he expected me to do that the bank couldn't do.

Should I call Jim now, or wait until morning? Should I call Drake first? I picked up my phone, still debating who I should call first. Without any further thought, I dialed Drake's number.

"Holly, what's wrong? Are you all right?" Even for a cop a late night call meant an emergency. Maybe especially for a cop, I thought.

For several minutes after explaining the strange call from Max, Drake didn't say anything. I pulled the phone away from my ear thinking the connection had been broken. Maybe I woke him up, and he needed to wake up enough to process what I'd told him.

"Why would someone frame him?" he finally asked.

"Maybe because he's an easy target," I suggested with a shrug in my voice. "You said it yourself he was a screw-up. People already suspect him." Especially Wally Miller, I added silently.

"Okay, I get that, but why did he call you instead of the police, or even Dad?"

"I don't know. He just said to tell Jim he didn't take the money, and to tell you to keep looking for the person who did. He didn't want you to assume he did it, and not look any further."

He gave a tired sigh. I could picture him running his fingers through his hair in frustration. "I wasn't going to assume anything. He should know that. The bank is trying to trace where the money was transferred to. I don't understand why he called you instead of calling me. What did he think you could do?"

That was a rather chauvinistic comment, but I kept that thought to myself. He's tired, or he wouldn't say something like that. At least I hoped he wouldn't. My conscience nudged me a little. I hadn't told him Max wanted me to help him. He certainly wouldn't like it. I could hear Drake's voice in my head without him even saying the words. *"Stay out of it, Holly. This isn't your job."* Like most cops, he wouldn't want civilians interfering in his investigation.

"I don't know why he called me instead of you. I'm just reporting what he said." Until I could figure out what Max expected me to find, I'd keep the rest of his request to myself.

"All right, thanks for letting me know. Get some sleep. I'll tell Dad he called. Don't tell anyone that Max called you."

I bristled a little. Just like that he was brushing me off? "I know how to keep a confidence. I'm not a gossip." We were both tired. We should leave it at that. But I didn't. "Are you going to tell your dad that Max called you?" I never figured him for someone who hogged the limelight, but I really didn't know him now.

There was a long stretch of silence again. Finally he gave a sigh. "I'm going to tell him what you told me. I don't want you…"

"For your information I wasn't planning on messing in your case," I interrupted, finishing his sentence. That wasn't exactly the truth. I'd be checking to see if there was anything I could find online. "I'm not a police officer."

"That's not what I said. Stop putting words in my mouth." We were both getting a little hot under the collar.

"Then what are you saying?"

"Well, if you'd stop interrupting, I'd tell you. You need to keep this to yourself. If someone really was hoping to frame Max, they aren't going to be happy that he called you, or anyone else. I'll tell Dad that Max called you, but don't be surprised when he hounds you to know what he said. For now, could you please tell him as little as possible? I don't want the real thief to come after either of you.

"Now I need to go. Get some sleep, and I'll talk to you in the morning." Before I could argue further, he hung up.

I flopped back on my bed. Why would he think the thief

would come after me simply because Max called me? How would coming after me benefit anyone? I fell asleep with these thoughts swirling around in my mind.

~~~

"Tell me exactly what Max said," Drake demanded. This was the third day he'd come to the library, pressing me for more information from my short conversation with Max. "Don't leave anything out." He was never satisfied with what I told him.

"I told you what he said that night and several times since then. How many times do we have to go over this? Why do you think I would hold something back? I want to help Max as much as you do."

"There you go again putting words in my mouth. I didn't say you were holding something back. Sometimes people remember something said days later. I'm just trying to make sure you haven't remembered something else." He ran his fingers through his hair, sweeping it away from his face.

Guilt pricked at me. I was still debating whether to tell him Max asked for my help. I wasn't sure what I was supposed to do though. "I'm trying to find him before the real thief does," Drake's voice broke in on my whirling thoughts. "That wouldn't turn out so well for Max."

He paused for a moment. "Were there any background noises, other people talking?" He kept pushing me to remember something, anything.

I closed my eyes, trying to recreate the phone call in my mind. "He was talking softly, almost in a whisper," I said. "I don't recall any other voices, but it was like he was afraid someone would hear him."

"Okay, that's good. What else? Were there any traffic sounds? Could you tell if he was inside or outside?"

Again I closed my eyes trying to recall any more details. "The call lasted no more than a minute. He said he didn't have much time. He sounded scared. I don't remember any other noise. I'm sorry, Drake. I just don't remember. What does the bank have to say?" I decided to change the subject. "How could anyone transfer the money out of the town's accounts without someone at the bank knowing about it?"

"They're working on it," he answered evasively. "Are you sure he didn't say anything else?"

This time I couldn't look him in the eye. My conscience was beginning to burn. "He asked for my help," I finally admitted sheepishly.

"What did he think you could do? You aren't in law enforcement, and you don't work at the bank."

"I don't know how he thought I could help. He just asked me to help." Did he think only the police and a bank could look into this?

"That doesn't make any sense. You're a librarian, not a computer expert."

"I know that. I'm just telling you what Max asked me to do."

"Why didn't you tell me that right away?" His fierce scowl would have been intimidating if I hadn't spent five of my growing up years with him. Besides, I didn't intimidate easily.

"Because I knew you'd have this exact reaction."

"Holly, you can't go poking into things. It could be dangerous. The bank is looking into where the money went."

"I'm aware of that. He was grasping at straws, looking for help from anyone he could. Drake, he was really scared." I put my hand on his arm, looking into his eyes. "I don't believe he took the money."

His big hand covered mine, his gaze softening as he looked down at me. "I don't want to believe he took it either, but what else am I supposed to think? He's the one who disappeared the same time the money did. He's the only one with the access codes. What else am I supposed to think?"

"You're supposed to keep digging until you find the truth. Maybe that's why he called me instead of you. He knows I'm just stubborn enough not to give up." I was getting tired of this conversation. If he wasn't going to keep looking, someone else had to. Maybe that someone was me.

"He should know I'm not going to give up without getting to the bottom of this, Holly." He sounded hurt that Max would doubt him. If I didn't know him better, I would think he was hurt that I could doubt him as well. "I want the town's money back as much as anyone."

"Good, then we can both work to find out who took the money." He started to argue, but I continued before he could say anything. "I promise I won't interfere with your investigation."

"That's not what I was going to say. If Max didn't take the money, someone else did. If that someone finds out you're looking into it, it could be dangerous for you."

"Well, I'm not stupid enough to advertise what I'm doing." The big doors swished open letting in the first round of students. "I really need to get back to work." The library was run by the town, but the building was on the high school grounds. Students spent a lot of time there before and after school when term papers were due.

As part of my job, I do a fair amount of research for anyone who needs help. I guess Max thought I could put that knowledge to work for him.

Max and the town's money had been missing for three days, and there still wasn't any information about what happened. People were getting tense. If the bank had found out where the money went, no one was saying anything. Someone at the bank had to know where the money had been transferred to.

Max hadn't called me again. Without hacking into the bank's records, I wasn't able to find anything. I had promised Drake and myself that I wouldn't do that. I had found out their security was seriously lacking though. Any teenager with average computer skills would be able to hack into their system. I had told Drake, but he didn't seem too impressed.

"Stay out of this, Holly. If you get caught with your fingers in the bank's business, I'll be forced to arrest you."

"I haven't done anything illegal," I bristled. "You aren't even listening to me. I'm not a computer expert, but if I found out this information, how long would it take for someone with better skills than mine to hack their system? Isn't it worth looking into? Maybe this is what happened to the town's money. Max might not have anything to do with it." The longer he was missing, the more people believed he was guilty.

"Then why did he disappear? If he's innocent, why won't he come forward?" I didn't have the answers, but I didn't want to believe Max would do what they were saying. He wasn't a thief.

When I got home that evening, my back door wasn't locked. I'd been in a hurry when I left, but I was sure I'd locked it. Maybe Bill had stopped by, and left the door unlocked, I told myself. Or maybe he was still here. There isn't a lot of crime in Pine Mountain, at least until recently, I qualified.

Pushing the door open, I remained outside ready to run if necessary. "Hello? Bill, are you here?" Everything I could see from my vantage point looked as tidy as I'd left it that morning. If someone had been inside, they hadn't destroyed anything in the kitchen.

When Max stepped into my line of sight, I sagged against the door I was holding open. "What are you doing here? How did you get in the house?" For some irrational reason I was whispering. My neighbors were far enough away that no one could hear me even if I screamed.

"I needed to talk to you, Holly. Has Drake figured out who did this? There should be plenty of clues. What's taking him so long?" He probably hadn't showered or shaved since this all began, and his clothes were dirty. It looked like he'd been in a fight. He held his side like his ribs hurt, and the bruises on his face looked fresh.

"Max, what happened to you? Who beat you up?" I stepped into my kitchen, touching his arm gently.

"Never mind that, I'll be okay. But you have to find where

the money is before they find me."

"Who are you talking about? If you know who did this, you have to tell Drake."

"No, I can't do that. With my background, no one is going to believe me. You have to find the guilty party." He paced around my kitchen.

"Me? Max, I can't hack into the bank files. Drake will arrest me."

"No, he wouldn't do that." He gave an aborted chuckle, grasping his ribs. "He loves you." That took my breath away.

"What are you talking about now? He has never said anything like that to me." We were getting far off track. He shook his head as if to dismiss that thought.

"Keep looking, Holly. I've left a trail for you to follow. I know you can do this."

"What trail? If anyone is going to find the money, it will be someone at the bank, not me. I don't work for the bank."

For a minute he looked worried about that. Giving a shrug, he turned back to me. "You're good with a computer." He pointed at my laptop on the desk in the corner. "You know how to look for things."

"What things? Max, you're talking in circles. I don't know what you expect me to do. I'm not with the police. If you know who did this, you need to tell Drake. How did you get in here?" Maybe there were more important matters to discuss, but I wanted to know if he had a key to my house.

He shook his head. "You really need to upgrade your locks. Anyone could get in with a credit card."

"Wonderful," I sighed. I hadn't thought it necessary to have locks like those needed in a large city. I turned my mind back to the issues at hand. "You need to turn yourself in. The longer you stay in hiding, the more convinced people are that you took the money."

"I didn't take it. You have to believe me. I haven't been the best brother, and I haven't always done the right thing. But I would never do something like this. I'm not like that anymore."

He continued to pace. "This wasn't supposed to happen," he muttered. "I can't believe I fell for their con. After everything I've done in my life, how could I fall for this? I'm not going to let them get away with it." As he paced around the room, he kept muttering to himself.

"Who, Max? Who are you talking about? You aren't making any sense. Tell me what's going on. You need to go to Drake."

"No, I can't do that. Not until I make this right. This will be the final con of the game. My last con," he finished softly. He stopped pacing, and turned to me. His face was intense, but scared. "You always were smart, Holly. I know you can figure this out if you keep looking. I've tried to tell you without getting you involved."

"But I will be involved if I look into this," I argued.

"I've stayed here too long already. I really need to go. Thanks for believing in me." He kissed my cheek, stepping towards the back door.

I grabbed his arm before he could leave. "Wait Max. What am I supposed to look for? Where am I supposed to look?" He shook his head. Whatever he was talking about, he was afraid to say anything more. "Please, don't go. Jim is worried about you. If you won't turn yourself in, call him. Let him know you're okay."

He kept shaking his head. "I can't do that, not until this is cleared up. Tell him I'm sorry, for everything." His eyes were moist now.

"What do you mean, for everything? Did you take the money?" My voice was harsh now. I didn't want to believe that, but like most of the people in town it was hard for me not to.

"No, Holly, no, I keep telling you I didn't take it. I would never do that. But it's my fault it's gone. I should have realized what they were doing before it was too late. Tell Jim I'm sorry. I didn't mean for this to happen. I thought it was

NEVER CON A CON MAN

just a game. This time the con man got conned. I've tried to protect myself as best I could. I won't let them get away with it, even if it's the last thing I do. This will be my last con." He kept repeating that. "You're smart, you'll figure it out." He pulled his arm out of my grasp, and disappeared out the door.

"Max," I called after him, but it was no use. He was gone. How was it his fault if he hadn't taken the money? For several minutes I debated whether to call Drake. I really didn't have a choice. If he found out Max had come to me, he would assume I was helping him get away. He might even think I was an accomplice.

Remembering Max's words that Drake was in love with me caused my breath to catch in my throat. Did he know what he was talking about? I had to put that aside for now. It was more important to find the money, and clear Max's name.

"What do you mean he came to see you? Why didn't you call me immediately?" Drake barked out the questions.

"I did call you immediately." My tone was as sharp as his. "He hasn't been gone five minutes."

"Where did he go?"

"Out the door. It's dark, and I couldn't see where he went once he was past the yard light. You do remember that the forest is in my back yard, right?"

He grumbled some more. "All right, I'll be right there." He disconnected the call without another word.

He showed up at my door a few short minutes later. He must have broken the land speed record to get here that fast. "All right, tell me what he said. Why did he come to you? Don't leave anything out this time either." His brows lowered over his light-colored eyes.

He already had my back up, and that comment didn't help. I tried to remember everything Max said, but his attitude wasn't helping. My mind was in a jumble. "He said he was sorry for everything." That was my leadoff comment.

"What does that mean? What was he talking about?"

"I don't know. He didn't explain, he just said he was sorry.

He didn't take the money, but it was his fault. I tried to get him to turn himself in, but he wouldn't listen to me."

"Did he say where he's been staying?"

"No, but I think he's living in the forest somewhere. He hasn't shaved or showered, and his clothes were dirty. It looked like he'd been in a fight. He kept holding his ribs like they hurt. He knows who took the money, and it has him really scared."

"If he knows who took the money, why won't he come to me with the information?"

"He said no one will believe him because of his past."

"Why did he come to you?" He always circled around to that point like he was jealous.

"I don't know." I shrugged. Drake was pacing around my kitchen the way Max had a short time ago.

"What's he going to do now?"

"I don't know. He said I was supposed to follow the trail, and I would figure it out. He kept say 'they' did this."

"What trail? How can you follow a trail if you don't know where it is? Who is this mysterious 'they'?"

"I don't know. I don't know. I don't know. He said the con man got conned. This was his last con."

"What's that mean?" Much the same as Max had done, Drake ran his fingers through his thick hair, mussing it up further.

"I. Don't. Know." I enunciated each word clearly. He wasn't listening to me. I wanted to take his shirt in my hands and shake him. Or kiss him. *Whoa. Where did that thought come from?* I took a step back to avoid temptation.

"What? You remember something." Drake gripped my shoulders, holding me in place.

"No. I didn't remember anything." *Including the fact that I need to keep some space between us,* I finished silently. *I almost did the unthinkable.* "I've told you everything he said. I don't know anything else." Did Max know what he was talking about when he said Drake was in love with me? I had to put that aside until we could find the money and prove Max was innocent.

CHAPTER THREE

Two days later the shrill scream of sirens filled the air as I made my way to the library. Police cars and an ambulance raced past me. Something bad had happened. Probably a car accident, I told myself. Motorcyclists liked to race on the mountainous roads. Sometimes they forgot to slow down when they entered the town. In the short time I'd been back in Pine Mountain, there had been one fatal motorcycle crash.

Turning the corner to the school parking lot near the library, all access was blocked off. Cars and students were lined up waiting to get into the lot. "Please, God, don't let it be one of the students," I whispered. Teenagers tended to think they were invincible, doing all sorts of crazy things.

Uniformed officers were milling around behind the library. If someone had broken in, as Head Librarian, I should have been called. But if it was a break in, why was an ambulance needed? I had a bad feeling about this.

Spotting Drake across the parking lot, I stepped out of my car. Walking up to the young officer manning the police tape, I tried to smile, but my face felt stiff. "I'm sorry, Holly, you need to stay out here." He spoke before I could say anything. He looked familiar, but I couldn't remember his name. He was about my age. If he'd lived here a long time, we'd probably gone to school together.

"I'm not trying to go anywhere, I was just wondering what's going on? Was there a break-in?" The badge pinned to his shirt said his name was J. Babcock.

"Um, ah, no," he stammered. His evasive answer caused my stomach to churn. He couldn't look at me when he answered. With this much police presence, it couldn't be good. Officer Babcock looked around, hoping to find someone a little further up the food chain to help him out.

"Did one of the students get hurt?"

"Um, that's not it. You need to stay here." He looked over

his shoulder again. Seeing Drake striding across the parking lot towards us, he gave an audible sigh of relief. I thought I might have heard a whispered "Thank God" in there.

"I'll take it from here, Jamie." Drake nodded his head, releasing him from guarding the tape perimeter. He couldn't disappear fast enough. I wasn't aware I was so intimidating. Or maybe it wasn't me. Drake didn't look very happy. A muscle in his jaw jumped as he gritted his teeth.

"What's going on? He said there wasn't a break-in at the library. Did one of the students get hurt?" I asked him the same question I'd put to Jamie. I was just getting to know the students, but those I had worked with were nice young people. I didn't want anything to happen to any of them.

Taking my arm, he led me away from the growing crowd of onlookers. "We found Max," he said softly.

"Was he hurt? What happened to him? I told you he was scared." I wasn't giving him a chance to answer, but I was afraid of what he was going to say. The look on his face said it all.

"I'm sorry, Holly. His body was discovered behind the library by two of the students." I covered my mouth to keep the gasp from escaping. My eyes burned with unshed tears. "It looks like he was recently in some sort of a fight."

"I told you he looked like he'd been in a fight." I couldn't wrap my mind around any of this. "Did he die from his injuries?" Guilt ate at me. I should have pressed him harder to turn himself in, to go to a doctor.

Drake hesitated for several beats before answering. "No. He was shot twice."

I could no longer hold in the tears that had been threatening. I swiped at them with my hand. Max was his uncle. This had to be harder on him than it was on me. "Does your dad know?"

He shook his head. "Not yet. I've been tied up here. I need to go tell him before someone else does." He looked over my shoulder, his mind on that hard conversation.

"Do you know who...did this?" I couldn't get the word murder past my closed throat.

"Not yet, but I will find out. I promise. I know you didn't believe he embezzled the town money, but..." His words trailed off.

"What? What aren't you telling me?"

"He had some money with him, a lot of it."

"That doesn't mean anything. It could be his money, not the town's. He needed money to survive until he could prove he was innocent." I didn't want him to be guilty.

Drake shook his head. "No, Holly, he wouldn't have that much cash on him."

"How much did you find?"

"At least ten thousand dollars," he said on a sigh. "A drop in the bucket when you think how much is still missing."

Ten thousand dollars wouldn't go far to keep the town running. Hopefully, Drake would be able to locate the rest of the missing money before long. "Why did he have that much cash on him?"

Drake shrugged his broad shoulders. "I don't have any answers yet. Hopefully, when we locate the rest of the money I'll have the answers I need." My heart went out to him. It couldn't be easy investigating his uncle's murder.

"We're going to be here for a while yet. I've already notified the school principal. The students and faculty will need to park somewhere else until we're done. You can open the library, but everyone will have to stay away from our crime scene."

He drew a ragged breath. "I need to go see Dad now." As he turned away his shoulders slumped with the weight of what he had to do next. I couldn't imagine having to tell someone his brother had been murdered. Watching him walk away, my heart went with him.

What was Max doing with ten thousand dollars in cash? Where would he get that much money? Unless he really had embezzled the money, the thought popped into my head. I quickly shook it off.

No, Max wouldn't do that to the town, or to Jim, I told myself. He had been scared when he came to see me. He'd done something he was sorry for, but I didn't believe it was embezzlement. I was convinced that he knew who took it though.

Within minutes people began speculating on who killed him. The embezzlement of the town's money offered a motive. But was it the real thief, or someone angry about the missing money? Wally Miller came to mind.

A ghoulish excitement settled over the students. The boys who found Max's body now had a macabre kind of celebrity. Teenagers don't look at murder and death the way adults do, I guess.

It was one of our busiest days since I started working at the library. Because I was still considered part of the Cox family, teachers and students alike came to me seeking answers and offering condolences. Unfortunately, I didn't have any answers for them, but I welcomed the sympathy. When Drake was able to make some kind of announcement, he'd call a press conference, or in the case of our town, a town hall meeting. Until then I was in the dark as much as anyone else.

Drake came into the library mid-morning to let me know the crime scene techs were leaving. "We're still going to be working there for a few more hours though. Until I can release the scene, people will need to stay away."

"Were you able to find anything to tell you who killed him?"

He shook his head. "It's going to take time to sift through everything." We had gone into the office so we wouldn't be overheard.

"This proves he didn't take the money, doesn't it?" I asked hopefully.

He shook his head, causing that lock of hair to fall over his forehead again. My fingers itched to put it back in place. I gripped them tightly to keep them from doing just that. "It just proves someone wanted him dead. Have you figured out what trail you were supposed to follow?"

It was my turn to shake my head, my chin-length hair sweeping against my neck. "I don't even know where to begin. How's your dad doing?" I changed the subject.

"He took it pretty hard. He had been telling himself Max wasn't a thief. With the money he had with him, people will be convinced he is though." He gave a weary sigh.

"No, Drake," I interrupted. "I don't believe that for a minute. You can't simply accept this as proof of his guilt. You have to keep looking."

"I'm not giving up, Holly. Someone killed him. I don't know if it was an accomplice, or because Max took the money, or someone else." His words echoed my earlier thoughts. He held up his hand when I started to object. "If he wasn't involved, why would he disappear at the same time as the money? Why would he have the cash on him?"

"I don't know, but I do know that he was scared when he came to see me. Now I have a question for you. How was the money removed from the accounts?" He looked at me, a blank expression on his handsome face. "Did someone take the money in cash?"

"No, there's no way someone could get away with several hundred thousand dollars in cash." I gasped at the amount missing. He continued as though I hadn't made a sound, "without someone at the bank being aware of it. The funds were wired out."

"So where did all that cash come from?" I continued to argue.

For a minute he seemed to consider my question. Then he shook his head. "I don't have any of the answers yet, Holly."

"Ten thousand dollars in cash, whether it's a deposit or a withdrawal, requires paperwork being filled out and sent to the IRS. Max would know that."

"The bank is looking into this, Holly." He kept telling me

that, but I couldn't let Max take the blame for something he didn't do. "I need you to stay out of this."

I ignored him. "All right, let's say you're right. Why would he stick around here if he had that much money? Wouldn't it be more logical for him to take off, just disappear for good?" I knew we were overlooking something important, but I didn't know what.

"I understand that you don't want to believe he's guilty. I don't either. But facts are facts." He was holding himself together with a strong will, but I could tell this was killing him inside.

His eyes lost focus for a moment as he considered all that was happening. "Wally is going to be all over Dad." The words came out so soft I wasn't sure I heard him correctly. "He's had a real hate going for Max for as long as I can remember."

That hate seemed like a good motive to me. Wally would do anything to discredit the Cox family, Max in particular. I'd been too young when I moved here to pay attention to the feud between the two men. As a teenager, I heard all the talk about how Max had stolen Wally's girlfriend. Even then I thought it was rather silly to be carrying a grudge over something that took place so long ago. Neither man had married the woman. I wasn't sure either of them even remembered her name. They just hated each other.

"Just because he had money on him when he died doesn't mean he's a thief," I said heatedly. Was I the only one willing to look past appearances, and try to find the truth?

"No, it doesn't, but I have to put emotion aside and look at the evidence. Right now that evidence is pointing to Max." He sighed. "I wish I'd had a chance to talk to him. I don't know why he didn't come to me with what he thought he knew." He was still upset that Max had come to me instead of him. There was nothing I could say. I didn't know what Max thought I could do that Drake couldn't.

On my lunch break, I walked down the street to the

hardware store to see how Jim was doing. Jim and Max's grandfather had started the store when he moved to Arizona as a young man. Both Jim and Max had worked there as teenagers. Max wanted no part of it as an adult, and couldn't wait to get away from the small town. When their father retired several years ago, Jim had taken it over.

"I'm so sorry about Max." For lack of anything better to say, I fell back on the old standby. I gave him a hug, hoping that would help in some small way.

"Thanks, Holly." He struggled to keep his composure. "People were convinced he took the money from the town, but I didn't want to believe he'd do such a thing. He wasn't always reliable, but I thought he'd changed. I don't want to believe he was a thief."

For several long moments he was lost in his thoughts. Finally he shook his head. "None of this makes any sense. At least we got part of the money back."

"If he took the money, what was he doing in town?" I asked, using the same argument I had with Drake. "If he really took the money, he could have gone anywhere. What was he doing behind the library?" I wasn't sure if Drake had told him that Max had come to see me. Was that something he wouldn't want anyone else to know?

Jim shrugged. "I have to leave this up to Drake. He has his hands full right now. There hasn't been a murder in town since…" He stopped, trying to remember. Finally he shook his head. "I can't even remember the last time there was a murder even close to town. Right now, I don't have any answers."

"Why didn't the bank do something before it was too late? Didn't they even check with you before the money was transferred?" He didn't understand what I was asking.

Before I could clarify what I meant, the door slammed open, hitting the wall and rattling the windows. "When is that damned son of yours going to tell us what the hell is going on? He wouldn't tell me if they found the rest of our money. There are bills this town needs to pay." Wally Miller was steamed up as usual.

Someone had leaked the fact that Max had money with him when he died. That was all the confirmation Wally needed to believe Max had taken the money. The amount found on Max hadn't been released, but that didn't mean anything to Wally.

Seeing me with Jim, he glared at me. "Aren't you one of Jim's step-kids?"

I shrugged. "I was, but I'm not now." I wasn't sure what this had to do with a murder and the missing funds, but Wally enjoyed having something to complain about.

He gave a sniff like there was a foul odor in the air. He turned back to Jim with another complaint. "You keep padding the town payroll with your relatives. Just because you're the mayor doesn't mean you can hire every rag tag relative that comes along. There are other people in this town who need jobs."

"Leave Holly out of this," Jim snapped. "There were no applicants with the qualifications she has." As long as they were arguing over my job, Wally wasn't blaming Max for the missing money.

"Did someone else apply for my job?" I asked mildly.

"My niece would like to have that job."

"Does she have a degree in Library Science? Has she ever worked in a library before?"

"That's beside the point." He waved me away like I was an annoying insect. "I didn't come here to talk about the library."

"You brought it up." I lifted one shoulder in a shrug.

With another glare in my direction, he turned back to Jim. "Has that son of yours found the rest of our money yet?"

"He has his hands full looking into a murder right now." A vein in Jim's temple throbbed with his attempt to keep his own temper in check.

"I don't give a damn about a murder. I want the money back. There are hundreds of thousands of dollars at stake here." By the way he was talking you would think it was his personal money that was missing. How much did he know about Max's death and the money he had with him?

Jim took a menacing step towards him, his hands balled into fists.

"Someone mind telling me what's going on here?" Drake stepped through the still open door.

Whirling around, Wally marched up to Drake, getting right in his face. "I want to know what you're doing about finding where our money is. What's taking you so long to find out where that damn uncle of yours put it?" The two men were standing nose to nose. Wally might have outweighed Drake by fifty pounds, but it was all fat. Drake was all muscle.

"I'm not in the habit of discussing an open investigation with civilians. I got a report that there was a problem over here. Want to tell me what's going on?"

"As a taxpayer I have every right to know what happened to our money." Wally puffed out his chest, edging a little closer to Drake.

"As soon as I have information that I can give out without jeopardizing the investigation, I'll report to the mayor and town council. They can inform the town."

"Your old man's the mayor, and he's standing right here. Tell him what happened to our money."

Drake's jaws were locked tight in an effort to control his temper. He was doing a better job of that than Jim. He was ready to explode.

"As I said, as soon as I have something to report, I'll do just that. Until then, I will continue to investigate."

"I have every right to know where that money went." He made the mistake of poking Drake in the chest with his finger, emphasizing each word. "I heard he had some of our money with him. How much did you find?"

Drake gripped Wally's hand, leaning over him like an avenging angel. "Unless you want to find yourself sitting in a jail cell, you'd better keep that finger in your pocket."

"You can't arrest me. I didn't do anything wrong." He was daring Drake to do just that.

"We can start with assaulting a police officer, and go from there."

Wally yanked his hand from Drake's grip, dropping it to his side. "I didn't assault you." He gave a sniff of disdain. "When I assault someone, it isn't a poke in the chest."

"Really? Care to elaborate on that statement a little? You assaulted anyone around here lately?" He lifted one eyebrow. "I got a dead body, and I'm looking for someone who made him that way. From the looks of the bruises on Max's body, someone had assaulted him within the past twenty-four hours. Your knuckles look pretty skinned up. Care to explain how that happened?"

"Go to hell."

"Already been there in Iraq, don't plan on going again. You want to come down to the station to explain those bruises?"

"If it's any of your business, I had an accident at work. You can't prove otherwise."

"We'll see about that. Now, I suggest you move along before you do something you'll regret."

With a few mumbled expletives, Wally tried to elbow his way around Drake. It didn't have the desired effect when Drake took hold of his arm, pulling him up close again. "I already warned you about assaulting an officer, Wally. You don't want to push much harder. I'm having a really bad day investigating my uncle's murder. I suggest you go back to work before I decide to haul your sorry ass to jail."

As soon as Drake released his arm, Wally rushed outside. When he was safely out the door, he must have felt brave once again. Giving Drake the one finger salute, he hustled to his truck that was parked at the curb.

"You didn't need to come to my rescue, son. I can fight my own battles. I was handling him just fine." Jim didn't sound grateful for Drake stepping in.

"I know you can handle him, Dad. But you two are like oil and water. Milly gave me a call when she saw him come in here. I don't need another murder on my hands right now." Milly Frazier owns the bakery across the street. She's old enough to be Jim's mother, and has always had a soft spot for the Cox brothers.

"Sorry, Son," He ran his hands through his hair. It was a gesture I'd seen Drake do many times when he was frustrated. His hands shook slightly as the adrenalin slowly left his blood stream. "Wally's been all over town grumbling about Max stealing the money. Maybe they got in a fight, and when Max couldn't tell him where the money was he decided to take the law into his own hands."

"Talk like that will only start another battle. Wally's a hot head, but I can't see him killing someone."

Jim's face got red, his temper on the rise again. "You don't know him the way I do. He's been blaming Max for everything bad that's ever happened to him."

"Dad, I need you to keep a cool head. Don't do something foolish."

Jim's shoulders slumped slightly, the fight gone out of him. "I'm not stupid, son. I have a little girl that still needs raising. Her mother…" He didn't finish his sentence. Jane wasn't exactly up for mother of the year. Clearing his throat, he changed the direction of the conversation. "I still think you might want to check out Wally's alibi for when Max was killed. Those two have hated each other for more than twenty years."

Wally owned the only construction company in Pine Mountain. He would drive fifty miles out of his way to get supplies to avoid shopping at Jim's hardware store. That was carrying a grudge a little too far if you asked me.

"I'll be checking out alibis for a lot of people. I want the person who did this, too. I also want to find the rest of the money that was stolen."

An accident on a construction site could explain the

bruises on Wally's hands. They could also be from a fight. If he thought he could bully Max into returning the money, I didn't think he'd hesitate to use force to get his own way. He'd been in more than one bar fight when I lived here years ago. It didn't appear that his temper had mellowed any with the passage of time.

"I need to get back to work," I said. "If there's anything I can do for you, let me know." I placed a kiss on Jim's cheek. "I really am sorry about Max. I was just getting to know him. It seemed like he had gotten his life together."

"Thanks, I appreciate that. I just wish we could prove that Max didn't steal that money." He gave a sigh.

"Working on it, Dad," Drake said. "I'll see you later." He followed me out of the store, draping his arm over my shoulders. My breath hitched in my throat at the casual yet somehow intimate contact. "What was Wally yammering about the library when I walked in?"

I was surprised he'd heard that. I didn't know how long he'd been outside the store before making his presence known. "He isn't happy that I got the job at the library. He seems to think his niece should have the job."

He chuckled, probably for the first time all day. "His only niece is seventeen and a senior in high school. I really doubt she'd thank him for suggesting she work at the library."

I tried not to take that as an insult about my career choice. Instead I changed subjects. "If Max really took the money, why didn't he transfer it to a numbered account somewhere? Why haven't they been able to find out where it was transferred to?"

"They're investigating the matter." That was his standard answer.

I held up my hand to stop him. "I know this is an open investigation, and you can't comment. Thank you for stepping in when you did. They were both ready to exchange blows. I'll see you later."

Turning away, I headed back to the library. I could feel his eyes on me as I crossed the street. I wasn't sure what he was thinking. My mind was spinning with unanswered questions. There was several hundred thousand dollars still missing. How could anyone get away with that much money without someone being aware of what was going on? Why hadn't the bank been able to trace the wire transfer?

As the town treasurer Max had access to the accounts. But he would know that taking the money in cash would raise all sorts of red flags. Had someone at the bank been working with him? Or had someone tried to frame him like he said? So why did Max have ten thousand dollars on him when he was killed? Why did the killer leave behind that much money? None of this made any sense to me.

When did the embezzlement first begin? If someone had been doing this systematically over a period of time, why hadn't anyone noticed? Or had the money disappeared in one lump sum? Again, why hadn't anyone noticed? Weren't there any safeguards on the accounts? How could I find out something like that?

A wire transfer to another bank would be easy to trace. After several more transfers, it would be nearly impossible to trace. Max was smart enough to know this. Why did Max have so much cash with him when he was killed? Why didn't the killer take it? The only explanation I could come up with was it had been left there in an effort to make Max look guilty.

To help pay my way through college, I had interned part-time at a bank, working in several different departments. Maybe I could put what I'd learned to use now, and try to figure this out. If someone at the bank had a hand in the embezzlement, the bank officials wouldn't want that made known. Most banks were willing to fire an employee for stealing and not report it rather than get a reputation for being an easy mark.

I'd only been back at my desk a few minutes when the library door opened again. With the heavier than usual traffic, I assumed it was another person looking for a tidbit of gossip.

I didn't realize how right that assumption was until Beth Ann Rodgers stopped in front of my desk.

"I was so sorry to hear about Max this morning, Holly. I know how close you are to the family. How is Jim holding up?" Beth Ann had been a year ahead of me in school. She had teased me about having a crush on Drake the entire five years I'd lived here. She had always enjoyed sharing any little tidbit of gossip she could repeat.

"As you can imagine he's very upset." I let it go at that. She had missed her calling. Instead of working at the bank, she should be working at one of those gossip rags at the grocery store checkout counter.

"Oh, yes. It's just terrible. Will Jane be coming home for the funeral?" Her full lips twitched like she had a secret she was dying to tell.

"I don't know what her plans are." She was as bad as the reporters when they stick a microphone in front of someone who has just tragically lost a loved one to ask how they're feeling. She took delight in knowing tidbits about people that she could exploit.

"Well, I'd better get back to work. We've been really busy lately." Were they extra busy because of the embezzlement, or something else? I still thought there had to be an inside person to facilitate the wire transfer.

As she passed the front desk where my assistant, Linda Hansen, was helping a student, she stopped. A sly grin curled her lips. I wasn't sure what that was about.

The remainder of the afternoon passed in a whirl of activity. Everyone wanted to know the latest on the murder. They all went away disappointed. I didn't know any more than they did.

I'd only been home a few minutes when Bill was at my door. He looked as though he was still in shock at the news of Max's murder. "How could something like this happen?" It was a rhetorical question, and I didn't try to answer. "I haven't had a chance to talk to Drake. What did he have to say?"

Everyone assumed that Drake would confide in me.

"Just that Max had been shot. I'm sorry, Bill." His arms closed around me when I stepped in to give him a hug. For a long moment, we took comfort from each other. He held on a little longer than necessary though. When it became awkward, I moved out of his arms.

"Max didn't take the money, Holly. I'd bet my life on that." He sat down at the kitchen table, holding his head in his hands.

"Please don't put it that way, Bill. Whoever killed Max is still out there. If he thinks you know anything about the embezzlement, he might come after you, too."

"You're worried about me, but you aren't worried about Drake?" He was suddenly angry. "Don't you think I can take care of myself?" There had always been a rivalry between the two brothers. I didn't want to get caught in the middle of that now.

"I don't want anything to happen to either of you, but it's Drake's job to investigate this." I paused for a moment, remembering the way Max had looked when he came to see me. "You're in the forest every day. Have you seen Max since he disappeared?"

"No, if I had I would have told him to turn himself in to Drake. Why would you think I'd seen him?"

"He came here a few nights ago. He looked like he'd been sleeping outside. Can you check around to see if you can find where he was hiding? That would be a big help to Drake's investigation." Giving Bill an opportunity to help with the investigation might avert more trouble between the brothers. Or it might cause even more trouble. Drake took his duties as police chief very seriously, as he should. But at times, he carried it to the extreme.

"I have a few days' vacation coming. I'll start first thing tomorrow." He was gone before I could stop him. I hoped he'd be careful. He was more impulsive than Drake. If he did find something, I hoped he'd take it to Drake instead of going after the person who killed his uncle on his own.

~~~

"You killed him? Why would you do that?"

"I didn't have a choice. He was going to tell what we did. He said he wasn't going to let us get away with this."

"Did he know about us?"

"I don't know." He shook his head.

"How did he know what we did? You said no one would figure it out. Why did you have to take everything at once?"

"Because he was going to turn us in. He figured out what we were doing."

"How did he do that?"

"He's good, that's how." A heavy sigh came over the telephone line. "Or he was good. He can't hurt us anymore."

"I thought you had everything under control. Do you think he told Holly anything when he went to see her?"

"I don't know what he told her, but I plan on finding out. Max said we did a good job of conning him, but he was better."

"Can't we just leave town? If you stopped him from telling anyone about what we did and taking our money, we can still get away. They won't know where to look for us."

"Are you sure you want to do that? You know what you'd be losing. Besides, if we leave right now, it would draw unwanted attention. We have to wait."

"No one was supposed to get hurt. How did it go so wrong?" There was no answer for that.

CHAPTER FOUR

The day before the funeral, Jane returned, looking full of concern for her husband. She swept into the library in a cloud of designer perfume, dressed like she'd just come off the runway at a fashion show. Carrying Hannah over to my desk, she sank down on the edge of the chair. I wasn't sure why she had come to see me. Shouldn't she be with her husband?

Her first words answered my unasked question. "Could you watch Hannah for me?" She was holding the baby away from her like she was afraid the smell of the dirty diaper would get on her fancy clothes. "I really need to go home and shower before I go see Jim. It was an exhausting drive, and the baby squealed most of the way. I don't think Jim needs a crying baby at this time. It's just terrible about Max. I can't imagine how Jim is handling this. It's bad enough that Max stole the town's money, but now someone murdered him."

"We don't know Max stole the money." I bristled at her automatic assumption that he was guilty. I was convinced he hadn't done that. I just couldn't prove it. I was still looking for the trail he said I needed to follow.

"Oh, I know." She waved that away like it meant nothing. "But who else would have taken the money, if it wasn't Max?" She stood up, holding Hannah out. It was either take her, or let Jane drop her on my desk. "I'm sure you don't mind watching her. I know how much you love her." This wasn't the first time she'd brought Hannah to me at the library expecting me to watch her.

"Thanks, Holly. I really appreciate this. I know Jim will as well." She placed the diaper bag on top of my desk, and swept out the door. In dumbfounded silence, I stared at her retreating back.

If she was so worried about her husband, why did it take three days after Max was killed for her to come home? Denver wasn't that far away. Putting that aside, I looked down at

Hannah. "What am I supposed to do with you, Sweetie?" She squirmed in my arms. Her little face was flushed, and when I tried to set her down on top of my desk, she stiffened, arching her back. How long she had been confined to her car seat with a dirty diaper? Some people shouldn't be allowed to have children. Jane was one of them.

Besides the hardware store, Jim and Max had inherited a hundred-acre ranch outside of town. Jane had to pass right by there on her way into town. If she was in need of a shower that badly, why hadn't she stopped there before bringing Hannah to me?

Of course, that would mean she would have to change the dirty diaper and watch the baby herself. From everything I'd seen since being back in town, Jane did as little of that as possible. There had been a succession of teenage girls that helped her out over the summer. Now that they were back in school, she was on her own. It looked like I was her next choice as a babysitter.

Linda's face was an angry red when I went to the front desk with the fussing baby in my arms. "It's high time she came back," she whispered. "But why did she leave the baby with you?" There was no love lost between Jane and Linda.

Linda was fifteen years older than me. She had been working at the library since I was in high school. I remembered that she'd been married once, but her husband had died shortly after they were married. As a teenager, I always thought she had a crush on Jim. Things hadn't changed on that score. She hated the much younger woman married to the man she was in love with.

After Jim and Mom were divorced, she might have been hoping Jim would notice her. Instead, he had stayed single until he met Jane two years ago. Linda didn't try to hide her feelings for Jane now.

"She said she needed a shower before she went to see Jim." I couldn't look her in the eye when I made the excuse. There was a lot more I wanted to say, but that would only fuel her hatred towards the younger woman. "I need to change her diaper. I'll be right back."

Placing Hannah on the counter in the ladies room, I stripped off the soaking wet and dirty diaper. I gasped at her red bottom. "You poor thing. It's no wonder you didn't want to sit down," I said in a cooing voice. "I wouldn't want to sit in that mess either. I bet your bottom hurts." With as many babies as my parents had over the years, I was more than qualified to care for Hannah. At least better qualified than Jane appeared to be, I thought. That didn't mean she should just drop her off when it was convenient for her. I was going to have to put a stop to this now, or it would only get worse. I felt sorry for Hannah though.

With a clean diaper and salve on her bottom, Hannah was happy again. She didn't want to be confined though. There was a children's area in the library, but it wouldn't do to turn an eleven-month-old loose in there. My phone was ringing when I got back to my desk. "Pine Mountain Public Library, this is Miss Foster. How may I help you?" I bounced Hannah on my hip while I cradled the phone between my ear and shoulder.

"Did I see Jane pull out of the library parking lot a few minutes ago?" Jim's voice held a world of frustration.

"Yes." I didn't need to say any more. Hannah's baby chatter told him why Jane had been at the library. "Didn't she stop at the store to let you know she was back?" I asked.

"No, I guess she didn't think it was necessary. I'll be over to get Hannah as soon as I can. Right now there are several customers in the store, and I'm alone. I'm sorry about this, Holly."

Jim had two employees, but they didn't work full time. He also had a couple of high school boys who went in after school. They wouldn't be there for another couple of hours. "It's all right, Jim. She'll be fine until you can get here. There's no rush." Replacing the telephone in its cradle, I looked down at Hannah. "What am I going to do with you?"

She smiled up at me around the thumb she'd stuck in her mouth. Rummaging around in the diaper bag to see if there was anything for her to eat, I came up empty. "Did Mommy even feed you?" It looked like it didn't matter. With a clean, dry diaper, her eyes were beginning to droop.

I couldn't imagine Jane driving all the way from Denver to Pine Mountain in one day, but I didn't think she would want to spend the night in a hotel alone with the baby either. She wasn't much of a mother.

Carefully spreading a blanket from the diaper bag on the floor, I laid Hannah down. She was asleep within minutes. She was still sleeping an hour later when Jim hurried across the lobby to my desk. "I'm sorry about this, Holly." He looked around for his daughter. "Did Jane come back for Hannah?"

I gave a soft chuckle. "No, she's asleep under my desk. Hasn't Jane been to the store to see you?" A frown creased my forehead.

A mask fell over his face in an effort not to show his disappointment in his young wife. "She's probably unpacking from her trip. She was gone longer than expected."

Or taking advantage of being without a baby to care for, and taking a nap, I thought. "You can leave her here if you'd like," I said instead. "We'll be closing soon anyway. If she wakes up before that, I'll give you a call."

"I hate to impose on you like that, Holly." He seemed torn between doing as I suggested, and seeing his daughter.

"I don't mind helping *you* with her." I hoped I hadn't put too much emphasis on the one word. "She's a good baby, and no trouble."

"I wish her mother…" He stopped himself from saying more. "Thanks for this, Holly. I really appreciate it. Give me a call when she's awake." Placing a kiss on my cheek, he turned to leave. His shoulders drooped as though the weight of the world rested there.

I couldn't help but feel sorry for him. He'd gotten himself in a jam when he married Jane. I hoped he'd been wise enough to have her sign a pre-nup before they got married. If not, I feared for his family ranch when, not if, she decided she'd had enough of small town living. In my estimation, she had married him looking at what was in it for her.

The library closed at five on most days. With the last customer gone, I walked across the tile floor to lock the door. Drake pushed it open before I got there. "Sorry sir, the library's closed for the day," I teased. Linda had left a few minutes before, so I wanted to keep things light between us.

"Very funny. I just came to check how things were going. I heard Jane dropped Hannah off for you to take care of." He shook his head, a lock of sun bleached hair dropping into his eyes. "Did Dad come get her?" He looked around for her now.

"She fell asleep so I told him to leave her here. She should be waking up pretty soon." As if on cue, we heard fussing coming from my desk. Before we got to her, Hannah had crawled out of the knee hole. Her lower lip quivered as she looked around at the strange surroundings.

"Hey, there Sweetie. Did you have a good nap?" Her big blue eyes were liquid with unshed tears. We stooped down so we weren't looming over her.

Drake picked her up, settling her on his arm. "Oh, um, I hope Jane left some diapers." There was a wet spot on the sleeve of his uniform shirt when he held her out to me.

Her laughter bubbled up at him. "You want the honors this time?" I asked. "I changed a dirty diaper when Jane dropped her off."

His face hardened. "She has no business having a baby. It was just a way to rope Dad into marrying her." That made me wonder if Jane had been pregnant when they got married. "When she leaves here, I'm going to make sure she leaves this one behind." He nuzzled Hannah's neck making her giggle. I noticed he said when, not if, she left here.

Picking up the diaper bag, I reached for Hannah. "It won't take but a minute to change her. We'll be right back." She giggled again when he tickled under her chin. Instead of staying by my desk as I expected, he followed beside me.

He stood in the doorway to the Ladies' room holding the door open. Since we didn't have to worry about any library patrons needing the facilities, I decided not to object. I was certain he'd changed a diaper or two. Jane would be glad to let anyone have diaper duty so she didn't have to.

When I pulled the tape off the diaper, Hannah braced her feet on the counter, lifting her bottom off the wet surface. "What happened to her bottom?" He stepped up beside me.

"Diaper rash," I said, trying not to make a big deal out of it. In fact, it was looking a lot better since I put the salve on it.

"That isn't normal, is it?" Although Jim had been married several times and had more children after Drake, he didn't have the experience with babies that I did.

"No, she sat in a dirty diaper for a while on the drive back from Denver. By tomorrow at this time, it will be all gone." If Jane keeps her dry and uses the salve, I silently qualified. A muscle in his jaw jumped when he clenched his teeth to keep any unkind thoughts from pouring out.

Jim was standing at the locked doors when we came out of the restroom. His face lit up when he saw Drake was holding Hannah. Jane might be immune to her daughter's charms, but she had her daddy wrapped around her little finger.

"Hi there, Pumpkin." He took her from Drake, nuzzling her neck much the same as Drake had done a few minutes ago. "I've missed you."

"Dada," she responded to his cooing voice, reaching out to pat his face. I thought he was going to melt into a puddle right there. I hoped for her sake, when one of them decided to end the marriage, Jim got custody of Hannah. Otherwise, she would be sadly neglected.

"Where's Jane?" Drake asked. His tone left no doubt about his feeling for the woman. "Did she even bother to come see you?"

"Don't start, Drake," Jim warned. "We've been over this before." The muscle jumped in Drake's jaw again, but he kept further thoughts to himself.

Grabbing my purse, I followed them outside. The wind had picked up since the morning, and the air had a chill that cut to the bone. I rummaged in the diaper bag for a sweater for Hannah. Not finding one, I wrapped the blanket she'd slept on around her until Jim could get her in his pickup. "She's going to be hungry," I told him. "I didn't find anything in the diaper bag for her to eat before she fell asleep." The muscle in Jim's jaw jumped now, but he didn't say anything.

As he was putting Hannah in the car seat, Jane's sports car pulled into the library parking lot. She rushed over to him, all mushy and full of apologies. "I'm so sorry, darling." She leaned towards him for a kiss, but he pulled away. She ignored Hannah.

"Where've you been?" Jim asked, stepping away from her.

"I didn't want you to see me the way I looked after that long drive, so I went home to shower. I lay down for just a minute to rest, but fell asleep instead. I just woke up. I'm so sorry." Hannah was used to being ignored by her mother, and didn't seem to mind now.

"So you left Hannah with Holly?"

"I know how hard Max's death has been on you. I didn't think you'd want to see her when she was fussy."

"I always want to see her." His manner softened only slightly when her eyes teared up. I didn't know how she could produce tears on command.

Jim turned away from his wife when Hannah began to fuss in her car seat. "She's probably hungry. You didn't have anything in the bag so Holly could feed her." It sounded like an indictment. Jane stiffened at his words, but was wise enough not to argue. "Thanks for taking care of her, Holly," he said. Placing a kiss on my cheek, he avoided making eye contact with his son, knowing what he would see there.

It was a twenty minute drive to their ranch, and instead of making the baby wait any longer for something to eat, Jim pulled across the street to the diner. Dennis and Darlene had three small grandkids and a menu especially for the little ones. Jane didn't bother to thank me for watching Hannah when she got in her car following Jim's pickup across the street. Did she realize she'd made a big mistake with her husband?

"I don't know what he was thinking when he got caught in her web." Drake shook his head as though shaking off a bad dream. "I'm hungry, but I'm not going to the diner as long as she's there with Dad. I've had all I can take of her for one day. Care to join me at The Steak House?" With only three real restaurants in town, there weren't a lot of choices. Fast food didn't count as a meal in my book.

"How about coming to my place? I can stop at the market and pick up a couple of steaks to bar-b-que." It would give me a chance to find out if he'd learned anything more about Max's murder.

Following me through the store, Drake placed a six pack of beer in the cart next to my bottle of wine. I'd gone in for steaks and ended up with a shopping cart full. "My treat," he said, pulling his wallet out before I could stop him.

My face got red when June, the cashier, chuckled. "Let's get together sometime," she said, a broad smile on her face. "Jill and I would love getting together for a girls' night out." The twins had teased me about my schoolgirl crush on Drake when I'd lived her before. It looked like she was going to start in again now.

Over the years our communications were mostly e-mail, Facebook and the yearly Christmas cards. When I came to visit we made a point of getting together. After moving back, we had renewed our friendship as though the intervening years hadn't happened.

"You didn't need to pay for everything," I said once we were outside. "I offered to cook." I didn't want a simple dinner to turn into something more like a date.

"I know, but I'm glad you asked. We haven't spent much time together in the last week." His eyes clouded over. The murder was still very real to him.

CHAPTER FIVE

Max's funeral turned into a fist fight. Most of the people attending came to support Jim, not out of love for Max. Jim had just stood up to give the eulogy when the door of the church slammed open.

"Don't go sayin' anything good about that bastard." A gasp swept through the congregation at his curse. "He deserves to rot in Hell for what he's done to me and to this town." Wally was drunk. It always came back to Max stealing his girlfriend in high school. Anything else Max did came second.

"Enough of that kind of talk, Wally." Pastor Ned walked down the aisle towards him. "This is the house of God. You need to leave."

Jim brushed past the pastor, his fist connecting with Wally's jaw. He staggered backward several steps then rushed at Jim with his head down like a bull ready to charge. Drake and Bill, along with several others pulled the two men apart. "That's enough. You're both under arrest." Drake's loud voice boomed in the suddenly quiet room.

"Why are you arresting me?" Wally slurred. "He attacked me first."

"You can't arrest me. I'm your father." Jim spoke over Wally's objections.

The muscles in Drake's jaw worked as he fought to control his temper. "You're both coming with me," he managed to ground out.

"I gotta go to work." Wally wobbled while several men gripped his arms to keep him from falling down.

"But this is my brother's funeral," Jim objected.

"You both should have thought of those things sooner." With Bill's help, he dragged Jim and Wally out of the church.

For several long moments there was complete silence in the church. Jane stood up, marching down the aisle after

Drake. "I've never been so humiliated in my life. He's going to pay for this." She didn't say who was going to pay.

"Folks, please take your seats," Pastor Ned tried to regain control of the situation. "Let us pray." There was a lot of shuffling around as everyone tried to take their seats and remember why we were there.

"Lord, please take charge of this situation we find ourselves in today. I pray that Max is now resting in your arms. Bless and bring comfort to his family. In Your name, Amen. This concludes the service. The family asked me to issue an invitation to a reception in the basement. Go in peace."

This wasn't how a funeral was supposed to go, but it was what we were left with. No one, least of all the family, felt like attending a reception luncheon, but we dutifully made our way downstairs.

"I'm so sorry this happened on today of all days." Jill Davidson gave me a hug. "My dad said Max and Wally never got along even as young boys. Wally blames Max for every bad thing that ever happened to him."

"I know." I nodded. "It looks like he's going to start blaming Jim now." I didn't know what else to say.

Jane had disappeared, whether she went to the jail after Jim, or she went home, or somewhere else, was anyone's guess. One thing I was sure of, she hadn't picked up Hannah from the church nursery. She left that up to me.

Holding Hannah now, I looked around the large room. People were standing in small groups or sitting at the tables picking at the food from the buffet. This funeral would be talked about for years.

"Has Drake said anything to you about who took the money and who..." It wasn't necessary for her to finish her sentence. I knew what she was talking about.

I shook my head. "Drake doesn't keep me informed about the case, and I'm trying to steer clear."

"You aren't doing a very good job of that," she chuckled. "The whole town knows you were buying groceries together the other day. Want to tell me what that was about?"

"It wasn't what it looked like." I'd forgotten how small towns loved to gossip. It was the one thing I hadn't missed when I moved away.

"It looked like you were fixing dinner for him." She gave me a teasing smile.

"Okay, so it was what it looked like. But it's not what you're hinting at. Jane dropped Hannah off at the library when she got home from her trip. Drake came over to check on her. After Jim took Hannah, I invited Drake over for dinner. I was hoping to find out if he'd learned anything new."

"And how did the dinner go?" She cocked her head to one side, giving me a knowing smile.

"The food was fine, the information sharing," I shrugged, "not so much. Drake is very one-sided when it comes to sharing information about an investigation." I sighed. "The bank has to know something. There has to be some record of where the money went, and who authorized the transfer."

Silence fell in the room when Jim walked in, followed closely by his sons. "I want to apologize for what happened today," he began. "I let my temper overrule common sense." His face was red with embarrassment. He went around the room thanking people for coming.

"Where's Jane?" Drake looked around, taking Hannah out of my arms.

"I take it she didn't follow you to the jail?" He shook his head. "Well then, I don't know where she is," I sighed. "She didn't pick up Hannah when she left."

"Call me later." Jill winked at me, a teasing smile playing around her full lips.

"What was that about?" Drake frowned at me.

"Nothing, she just wanted me to call her later." I shrugged off his question.

"Where's Jane?" Jim echoed Drake's question when he and Bill joined us. He looked around for his wife.

"Um, she went home?" My voice rose at the end, turning

my words into a question.

"Of course she did. And she forgot all about Hannah." He looked bone-weary.

"Dad," Drake and Bill spoke at the same time.

"Not now, boys. I've had enough for one day." Taking Hannah from Drake, he left the reception hall.

"When's he going to wise up and dump that broad?" Bill spoke quietly. "She doesn't care about him or Hannah." This was the one subject they agreed on.

"That's something he's going to have to decide for himself," I sighed. "It's not up to us to make that decision for him." Although I want to, I added silently.

"Did you really arrest them?" I looked at Drake.

"I couldn't arrest Wally for drunk and disorderly, and let Dad off on assault," he heaved a sigh. "I gave them both a warning, and let them go. I'm not sure Wally will even remember the incident when he sobers up."

"I hope he doesn't go to work like that. He could hurt himself or someone else."

"I sent him home with one of my officers," he said. "As drunk as he was, he'd crash into a tree."

This was the first time I'd seen Bill since the day he came to my place after Max died. I wanted to ask if he'd found anything in the forest to suggest Max had been staying there. I knew Drake wouldn't approve of either of us interfering, so that would have to wait.

The three of us made the rounds, thanking everyone for coming, and left as quickly as possible. It had been a long week for all of us. It wasn't going to get any better for Drake until the killer was found, and the money returned.

Unless irrefutable evidence was presented, I wouldn't believe Max had stolen the money. It was my theory that the embezzler killed him to keep him from talking. Max said he knew who did it. Why didn't he tell Drake? Or me, I thought. He'd come to me, so why not tell me? I wished he had told me more the night he came to see me. I still didn't know what he expected me to do. I didn't know what trail I was supposed to follow.

~~~

"How did this happen?" she whispered. "I didn't sign up for this. It was supposed to be easy. No one was supposed to get hurt. We were going to get the money and disappear."

"I know, but things changed."

"How? Why?"

"Um, it's gotten a little more complicated." He paced away from her.

"What are you talking about?"

"Max wasn't as dumb as we thought."

"What's that supposed to mean?" She glared at him. "I want out. Now."

"Soon, I promise." His voice trembled slightly, putting the lie to his words.

~~~

Drake's SUV was parked outside Jim's hardware store when I drove through town the next morning. Instead of going directly to the library, I made a detour. I wanted to know if Drake had made any progress on the case. The bank wasn't being very helpful. Jim opened the store early every morning, but they were alone when I walked in.

They were in the middle of a serious conversation, and ignored me. "I'm sorry, Dad," Drake said, drawing a deep breath before he continued. "Max was the only one authorized to make transfers." He was still trying to make sense of things.

"No, that's not right." I frowned at Drake.

He gave me a sad smile. "I'm sorry, Holly. I know what Max told you, and you don't want to believe he would do something like that. But he was the one with the authority to transfer money, especially that large of sum." He turned back to his dad. "The bank is trying to locate where the money was transferred to, but they aren't making much headway."

"You don't understand," I interrupted again.

Drake shot me a glare that was meant to shut me up. It

didn't work. "Just listen to me for a change. There had to be a backup in case Max got sick or was on vacation. Someone else in his office had to have the authority to transfer funds. Transferring large sums of money would probably require two people authorizing the transfer. At least that's the way it is with most large corporations. I don't think the town would be so lax as to have only one signer. Who was the second signer?"

"I already told you I spoke with Jack Johnston. He's the one who alerted us about the missing money."

"I'm betting he also had the authority to transfer funds," I argued.

Drake's sigh was weary. "If he embezzled the funds, why did he stay in town while Max disappeared? You're grasping at straws, Holly. They won't hold up."

"That may be so," I said defiantly, "But there had to be someone else authorized to transfer funds. It doesn't seem that people at the bank are being very cooperative."

"Stay out of it, Holly," he growled. Without another word, he stomped out of the store.

It would be interesting to know how Jack Johnston had felt when Jim hired Max instead of him as treasurer. Did he have an ax to grind? It might be worth checking into, but I wasn't sure how to go about it. Putting that thought aside, I turned back to Jim.

"I'm sorry." I didn't know what else to say.

"I know. I don't know what to believe. Max had always played a little loose with the rules, but I really thought he had changed when he came home this last time. I just don't want to believe he would do something like this."

"I don't think he did." Kissing his cheek, I went out to my car.

~~~

Two days after Max's funeral, Jim called another town meeting in the high school auditorium. His face was haggard, and it looked like he'd lost ten pounds since this began.

"First, I want to thank everyone for the condolences expressed after Max was…" He didn't finish that thought. Clearing his throat, he began again. "I wanted to keep everyone informed as much as possible." Drake was on the stage with him. I had my fingers crossed that he wasn't going to give up on the investigation.

"The bank is still trying to trace the money," Jim went on, answering one of my questions.

"You're damn brother stole it," Wally shouted.

"Sit down and shut up, Wally, or I will haul your ass to jail." Drake's harsh growl surprised Wally into silence. At least for a little while.

"As I said, the bank is still working on this," Jim continued as though there hadn't been any interruption. "It's taking time to discover who was involved." It shouldn't take this long to discover where the money had been transferred to, I thought. Drake didn't want to listen to me though.

"It doesn't take a mental giant to figure it out," Wally mumbled loud enough for people to hear. "Max screwed the town just like he screwed me years ago."

Jim placed his hand on Drake's arm when he moved towards the steps. "Don't, son." He drew a deep breath, letting it out slowly. "There is another matter that needs to be discussed."

"What else did Max do to hurt this town?" Wally didn't know when to let it go.

Drake didn't let his dad stop him this time. Walking down the steps, he made his way through the crowd. Before he reached the row where Wally was trying to hide, he scrambled over the people beside him, running out of the hall. People laughed, until Jim pounded the gavel on the table.

"Settle down, folks. We have business to discuss here." Again he drew a deep breath. "It seems that a big box store has been trying to gain ground here in town. They've been working behind the scenes, and it has just come to my attention. That would wipe out several stores, and could destroy our downtown area. I'm not sure that's something we should consider."

"Can't we all sign a petition to stop them?" Bud Walker stood up. Bud and his wife Arlene owned the only grocery store in town. "I couldn't compete with the prices of one of those stores. It would put me out of business."

"That will be the concern that all the store owners in town will have," Jim said. "The town council is working to put a stop to their plans."

"Is it a done deal?" Someone else shouted the question.

"As I said, I didn't learn about this until today. That's why the hastily called meeting. Before Max...died," Jim faltered before he got control of his emotions, and was able to continue. "He was working on stopping the store from moving forward with their plans. It's going to take time, but I'm confident that once the corporate offices learn that the town doesn't want them here, they will rethink their plans."

"Is that why he was killed?" The buzz went around the room. Once again Jim pounded the gavel to regain order.

"We're looking at every angle," was Drake's only comment.

"I'll bet Max was behind the deal to begin with," Wally shouted from the back of the room. He quickly ducked back out again before Drake could do anything.

I didn't want to believe a big corporation would have Max killed because he was trying to stop them from building a store in town. What, if anything, did this have to do with the missing money?

Fear that our way of life was about to be destroyed was written on the faces of everyone as they filed out of the auditorium a short time later. Drake had said very little during the meeting. Apparently he was there to maintain order, and make sure Wally didn't start another fight with Jim.

"What about that big store?" I asked softly as I walked out with Drake. "Would they really kill someone trying to stop them from building here?"

"The town council is working to figure out how deep the corporation has managed to worm their way into things around here." His sigh caused a cloud to form in front of his face in the cold night air.

Switching topics, I continued to press. "Who were they working with to get the proper authorization?" When he remained stubbornly silent, I asked another question. "Why hasn't the bank been more cooperative? Someone should be able to tell you where the money was transferred to. It's been more than a week now. Who authorized the transfer? Someone has to know something. I think they're trying to cover their own backsides." Drake let me rant without commenting.

Leaning against the door of my car, he watched me with hooded eyes. When I finally wound down, I sighed. "If you aren't going to tell me anything, please move so I can open the door. I want to go home. It's too cold to stand around out here." After living in Phoenix while I went to college, my blood had thinned. Seventy degrees was cold to me, and the temperature was a lot colder than seventy at the moment.

His dark gaze was trained on me, but he remained silent. It was a technique police used to get a suspect talking. I didn't know what he suspected me of, though. I finally clicked the key fob to unlock my door. "I'm cold, so I'm going home. Good night." He still didn't move.

"Drake, please move. I'm cold. I want to go home." Before I knew what he was going to do, he pulled me against his hard chest, wrapping me in his warm embrace. He rested his chin on top of my head. "Wh...what are you doing?" My heart was pounding in unison with his.

"You said you were cold. I thought I'd warm you up." I felt him shrug, but he didn't release me.

"Not out here where everyone can see us." My voice squeaked.

"So what if they do?"

"So tongues will be wagging by morning. You know what they're going to say."

"Why do you care what they say? We're both single and over twenty-one. And we're not related now." He knew what my next objection was going to be.

"People still look at us as brother and sister."

"People are wrong. Besides, that was a long time ago, and we were never blood related. There's nothing wrong if I want to do this." Putting his finger under my chin, he tipped my head up, placing a soft kiss on my lips. My arms had been pinned between us. When he lifted his head, they were wrapped around his waist, holding him close.

"Get a room." June had just left the auditorium. She gave a merry laugh and kept walking when we jerked apart.

"Not yet," Drake called after her, causing her to laugh harder.

"Darn it, Drake." I slapped his arm.

"What? You were enjoying that as much as I was."

"That's not the point. I just moved here. I don't want people gossiping about me."

"Okay," he shrugged. "Let's go to your place. Or mine," he added when I shook my head.

I wasn't sure how far he planned on this game going, but I wasn't willing to find out. My high school crush was still alive and well. I needed to keep my distance. I didn't trust myself.

Laughing, he opened my door for me to slip inside. Before closing it, he leaned down giving me another kiss that rocked me to the soles of my feet. I watched him in my rearview mirror as I pulled away. He didn't make any attempt to follow. I couldn't decide whether I was disappointed or glad.

A light rain began to fall as I made my way home. The temperature was dropping steadily. Snow was in the air. Thanksgiving was only a few weeks away. Then it would be Christmas and the New Year. No matter what family I'm with during the holidays, there is always a big celebration. I'm always thankful for everything God has given me. But this year it didn't feel like there was much to celebrate.

CHAPTER SIX

My lips tingled from Drake's kiss. I didn't know what to make of that little episode. Was he serious, or toying with me? He knew I'd had a crush on him in high school. Would he take advantage of that now? How well did I really know him? I willed my heart rate to slow down, but it wasn't listening to me. Someone had said "Your heart wants what it wants." In my case, my heart wanted Drake.

My mind was still struggling with these questions when I pulled into the driveway at my small house. Once again I'd forgotten to leave the outside light on when I left that morning. Away from the street lights in town, it was extremely dark. Still the moon and stars gave off enough light that I could see someone was sitting on my front porch.

My heart began pounding in my chest again, only this time Drake wasn't the cause. The shadows shifted when the person stood up, and my breath came out in a whoosh. Pushing open my car door, I stepped out onto the gravel drive. "Darn it, Bill. You almost gave me a heart attack. Why didn't you call to let me know you were going to be here?"

He lifted his shoulders in a shrug. "I came to see what happened at the town meeting tonight." He didn't come into town very often. He preferred being in the forest. In fact I hadn't seen him since the night of Max's funeral. I didn't know if he'd found where Max had been hiding. What if I'd guessed wrong because of the dirty clothes Max had been wearing, and sent him on a wild goose chase? I didn't know where else he could have been hiding though.

"If you knew about the meeting, why didn't you attend?" I asked, unlocking the front door, and holding it open for him. "I'm sure your dad would have appreciated the moral support."

"I'm not much for crowds. Besides, this gives me a reason to visit you." A smile tilted his lips up.

"You don't have to have a reason to visit me. Just call first, don't sneak up on me. You don't like crowds, I don't like surprises. We should both remember that." His face turned pink at my scolding tone.

"Sorry," I said, giving a sigh. "I have to discipline the teenagers in the library so often I tend to forget when I'm talking to an adult." Maybe it was also because he acted like a sullen teenager part of the time. I kept that thought to myself though.

"So, how did the meeting go?" He flopped down on the couch, propping his feet up on the cedar chest I used as a coffee table.

Moving his feet off, I sat down beside him. "Did you know that one of those big box stores is trying to build here?"

"No, I hadn't heard anything about that. That kind of store would ruin most of the small businesses in town." He shook his head. When he draped his arm along the back of the couch, letting it fall over my shoulders, I moved to put some space between us. "Dad doesn't need that on top of Uncle Max's murder and the missing money. Does that have anything to do with his murder?"

"I don't know." I shrugged. "Your dad just learned of it this morning. That's why he called the meeting. People needed to know what was going on. Jim said Max was trying to stop them from building here."

He sat up, frowning at me. "What did Drake have to say? Does he think that's why Max was killed?"

"You know he can't say much about an ongoing investigation, but he's looking at all angles."

"Yeah, right. He just wants to keep everything to himself so he can be the hero when he solves the case." He sounded bitter.

"Stop it, Bill. You know that isn't how Drake feels. He's just as concerned about finding the killer and the money as you are."

"Except he doesn't share any of his information with the

town, does he?" I wanted to tell him to stop acting like one of the teenagers in the library, but decided that would only make matters worse.

"You know he can't divulge information about the investigation. Were you able to find out where Max had been hiding in the forest?" Changing the subject seemed like a good idea.

"Yeah, there's an old shack a few miles from here. It looks like someone's been there recently."

"That's great. What did Drake say?" Maybe this was the trail Max had told me to follow.

His expression darkened. "I haven't told him. There wasn't anything there, just the empty shack." He shrugged his shoulders. "Big brother isn't going to like me sticking my nose in his investigation," he grumbled.

"You can't go looking for a killer by yourself, Bill. You need to tell Drake about that shack."

"So he can tell me to butt out? I don't think so." His jaw was set stubbornly. At that moment, he looked very much like his older brother.

He abruptly stood up. "I'd better get going. I'll see you later."

"Bill, please wait. Tell me what you found."

"So you can tell Drake?"

"What's that supposed to mean?"

"You always had a thing for him. I don't imagine that's changed any. Besides, Drake already knows about that shack. It's been there for years. We used to go out there as kids. It's in a lot worse shape now. If Uncle Max had been there, he didn't leave anything behind. It just looks like someone had been in there recently. I'll keep looking. If Drake doesn't think to go out there to find where Max was hiding, that's not my fault."

Trying to ignore the jealousy in his voice, I followed him to the door. I put my hand on his arm to stop him. "Please be careful. Whoever did this to Max won't hesitate to kill again if he thinks you're getting too close."

"Did you tell Drake that too? Or is that advice just for your little brother? In case you've forgotten I'm not that much younger than you. I'm all grown up now. And I'm not your brother anymore." Before I realized what he was going to do, he pulled me into his arms, pressing his lips against mine in a hard kiss.

Struggling, I pushed him away. "What are you doing?"

"I'm kissing you, but I suppose you'd rather have Drake instead of me." He slammed out of the house, disappearing into the dark forest.

I shut the door, resting my head against it. I didn't know what to do about Bill. I cared for him, but not the way he wanted. Drake was another matter. I was more than half in love with him, and probably always had been. He'd kissed me, but was this simply a game with him? Or did he care for me in the same way?

This wasn't getting me anywhere. I turned my thoughts to the night's meeting. When chain stores moved into a small town, it wasn't always a benefit to the town. Small businesses would close, and that would hurt a lot of people.

Jim said Max had been trying to stop the store from building in Pine Mountain. What would a corporation do if someone opposed them? Killing the opposition seemed a little extreme. There were other towns that would welcome a big store, just not ours.

What about the town's funds? Drake kept saying the bank was working on it. But what was taking so long? Someone had to know where the money had been sent. It wouldn't be hard for someone with good computer skills to hack into their system. Is that what happened? Is that why it was taking them so long to recover the funds?

If this was one of the major banks, it would be harder, but not impossible, to hack their system. As a small local bank, their system was less secure. There still had to be safeguards in place so things like this didn't happen. Transferring hundreds of thousands of dollars should require special authorization, maybe even two signatures. So how had it been done? I would love to see who had the authority for such a transfer. Emptying the accounts should have raised a red flag.

Someone else in the treasurer's office should have access to the codes. Drake said he'd talked to Jack Johnston. Had he checked him out? I shook off that thought. Of course he had. Drake knew his job. Max said he was to blame, but he hadn't taken the money. What did that mean?

What if the accounts had been hacked? Maybe security in the treasurer's office was as poor as that at the bank. That would mean anyone anywhere could have taken the money. All it would take was someone with good hacking skills. They could wipe out hundreds of accounts.

I fell asleep with these thoughts swirling around in my mind.

The next morning I decided to do a little digging of my own. I'd promised Drake I wouldn't hack into the bank. He said he'd arrest me if I did anything illegal, and I believed him. I couldn't talk to anyone in the treasurer's office, but there was nothing to stop me from asking questions about my own accounts at the bank. As long as I didn't ask about the town's accounts, I wasn't doing anything illegal.

I called Linda to give her a heads-up that I'd be late. Saturdays aren't very busy, and the library is only open until noon. She could handle things until I got there.

"Did that woman con you into watching her baby again? That poor little thing needs a mama who loves her, not just her daddy's money."

"Um, ah, no, this has nothing to do with Jane or Hannah." It didn't take a mental giant to know who she was talking about. Bill wasn't the only one with a jealous streak. "I need to run an errand. It shouldn't take me long. I'll be there as fast as I can."

I hung up before she started on another tangent. Linda had worked at the library when I lived here. I had been surprised when she hadn't applied for the head librarian position. I'd been afraid there would be some resentment from her, but she seemed happy doing what she did.

Forgive me for this little deception, Father. I said my prayer as I pushed open the bank door promptly at nine. *I have good intentions. I hope that counts for something.*

"Hi Beth Ann, how are you this morning." I hoped I didn't look as nervous as I felt.

"Holly, hi. What are you doing here? I mean, how can I help you?" Her hands shook as she picked up the pen on her desk.

"I need to speak to someone in your wire transfer department. Could you point me in the right direction?"

"Are you helping Drake find the town's money?" She leaned across her desk, her eyes nearly popping out of her head.

"Are you kidding?" My horrified gasp wasn't for show. "Drake would arrest me if he thought I was interfering in his investigation."

"No, he wouldn't." She gave a little laugh. "That man's been in love with you since you were kids. I bet you could do just about anything, and he wouldn't mind."

I could feel heat moving up my neck now, looking around to see who was close enough to hear her. "I think you're imagining things, Beth Ann. Drake and I are just friends."

"Friends with benefits?" She giggled like a school girl at that. By now my face felt like it was on fire with embarrassment.

"Could I speak to someone in the wire transfer department?" I needed to put a stop to this conversation before it went any further.

"Oh, um, sure, I'll take you. Fred is right down this hall."

It turned out that Fred was fresh out of college. Or maybe high school, I thought when I got a better look at the young man. He probably hadn't started shaving yet. I thought that was a little young to be working in a department with so much responsibility.

When it became obvious she wasn't going to leave, I smiled at her. "Thanks a lot, Beth Ann. I'll stop by on my way out. We need to get together for lunch sometime." That was another lie I needed to ask forgiveness for. Beth Ann wasn't one of my favorite people. Not only had she enjoyed teasing me, she had also manipulated people and situations. I doubted that had changed any.

"Oh, sure, that would be great. Take good care of her, Fred. She's the Mayor's step-daughter." She reluctantly shut the door on her way out.

"I...I didn't know Mayor Cox had any step-daughters," Fred stammered. I wondered if he was nervous because of Beth Ann's pronouncement, or because he'd done something wrong. "Isn't Jane...I'm mean Mrs. Cox too young to have a daughter your age."

Jane, huh? I thought. Just how well does he know her? I guess in a town the size of Pine Mountain, you know most of the people by their first name, even if you don't have a personal relationship with them.

"Actually, Jane and I are about the same age, and I'm not Jim's step-daughter any longer. He was married to my mom years ago. I have a few questions I would like to ask about having funds transferred to another bank."

"Are you working with the chief?" His Adam's apple bobbed up and down as he gulped. He gripped his fingers so tight the knuckles were white.

"No, why would you think that?" Maybe Drake needed to take a look this young man. Put a little pressure on him, and he might tell everything he knows.

"Oh, um, I thought since you're like Mayor Cox's step-daughter, um never mind. What do you want to know?" He finally managed to get his nerves under control.

"I'm supposed to get some funds wired into my account from an investment. Are there any papers I need to sign?" I'd spent six months in the wire department when I was interning at the bank in Phoenix. Let's see if he knows his business, or if things had changed much in the last few years.

He relaxed. "No, you don't have to sign anything when you're receiving a wire. Will it be a large sum?"

"Yes, well, large for me." I laughed. I was beginning to get nervous now. An old saying I'd heard as a child came to mind. "Oh what a tangled web we weave when first we practice to deceive." I didn't want to get caught in that web. "I'll be transferring it out again within a few days. Do I need to sign any forms for that?"

"Yes, I can get you all set up, and you simply need to call me when you're ready to make the transfer." He reached for some forms in a drawer. "Do you know how much you'll be transferring?"

"How secure is a wire transfer? There isn't any way someone can redirect the funds, is there?" I ignored his question.

"You mean like embezzling them?" His face had lost some of its high color now.

"Well, yes, I suppose that what I mean. I want to make sure it will be secure."

"A wire transfer is more secure than sending a check, and is done immediately. There is not hold placed on the funds at the other end either."

Nothing new there, I thought. Nothing incriminating either. "Do I need to have more than one signature to authorize a transfer?"

"Are you the only signer on your account?" He frowned at me. I nodded my head, afraid I'd gone too far with my questions. "As long as you are the only signer, it will only require your signature." He continued to frown at me.

"That's great. I just want to make sure it's secure. I don't want anything to happen to my money. It's all I have."

"If you're worried that someone on the other end will steal your money, maybe you should deal with a better investment company. I can assure you that your funds are extremely secure here. We have an investment professional here. Maybe you can talk to him. Then you wouldn't have to worry. Your money will all be in one spot." He had his sales pitch down pretty good.

"Let me think about that." I stood up to leave.

"What about signing the transfer forms?" His nerves had turned to suspicions now.

"Well, if I decide to invest through the bank, I won't need them. I'll let you know when the funds are going to be wired in. Thanks for the information." I quickly left the office. Making an appointment with an investment counselor was going a little farther than I had planned. I would get caught in my own lie for sure.

Stepping into the lobby, I stopped when an argument erupted between two men. Wally Miller was arguing with a man dressed in a fancy suit. Everyone in the lobby turned to stare at them. I couldn't hear all that they were saying, but there was no doubt that Wally was angry.

"I told…need to stop…" Wally's gravelly voice rose and lowered with the words, making it difficult to understand what he was saying. Fancy Suit managed to keep his voice low enough that others couldn't overhear what he said.

"Gentlemen, please, this is a business. I can't have you making a public display." The bank manager stepped between Wally and his opponent.

"That's too damn bad. These people can't come in here and take over our town." Wally shoved Fancy Suit out of his way as he stormed out of the bank. If there hadn't been an automatic stop on the door, he would have slammed it hard enough to break the glass.

Take over the town? I thought. Who was that guy? My best guess was he worked for the corporation wanting to open a store in Pine Mountain. It seemed a coincidence that someone from that corporation would show up so soon after Max's murder when he was trying to stop them.

Seeing me standing in the hallway, Beth Ann hurried over

to me. "Can you imagine Wally making such a spectacle of himself right here in the bank!" Her face was flush with excitement, belying her disgusted tone.

"That's always been Wally's way." I shrugged. I wasn't going to add to her gossip. "I have to get to work. I'll talk to you later." I hurried out before she could stop me.

Driving the short distance to the library, I mulled over what I'd learned from Fred. It wasn't much. The most interesting item was that Fred and Jane had some sort of relationship. But what kind? How well did he know her? They were closer in age than Jane and Jim were. Was that their only connection? He was certainly nervous about something. I decided to look him up on Facebook and other social media the first chance I got.

If he was like so many of the young people who frequent the library, he would be on several different sites. They never took into consideration that what you put on the internet today is there forever. Even the apps that are supposed to delete a message after a certain length of time can still be found much later, sometimes with unthought-of consequences.

Linda was busy helping a student when I arrived at the library. Her lips were compressed in a thin line when she looked at me. I didn't know if she was upset that I was late, or something had happened with a student. If she had something to say, it would have to wait until we were alone.

Watching a table of teenagers, their thumbs moved rapidly over the small keyboards on their phones. Were they looking something up, or chatting on one of the social apps they used? Spelling and communication skills were being rapidly destroyed by texts and social media. I worried about this generation coming up on adulthood. How were they going to manage without any social skills when they got out in the real world?

After locking up for the day, I stopped at Linda's desk. "I'm sorry I was late this morning. I hope it wasn't too busy."

"That woman came in looking for you. When I told her

you weren't here, she gave me the third degree, wanting to know where you were. I felt like telling her it was none of her business, but I held my tongue." Jealousy was getting the better of her.

"That woman?" I could guess who she was talking about.

"Yes, Jane Cox. She had that precious baby with her. She wanted you to babysit again."

"Oh." I wasn't sure what else to say. I should put a stop to this, but I felt sorry for Hannah. Left in Jane's care, she was neglected at best, and abused at worst.

"She uses you as her personal babysitter even though you work, and she doesn't. I don't know why Jim ever married her." I wasn't going to touch that topic. "I noticed she didn't attend the meeting last night either," Linda continued to rant. "She should have been there to support her husband."

"I guess she didn't have a babysitter since I went to the meeting." I meant it as a joke, but she took it seriously.

"Well, there are plenty of teenagers in this town," she huffed. "She could hire one of them for a few hours. Hannah would be better cared for by a teenager than by her own mother."

She drew in a deep breath letting it out slowly. "I'm sorry, Holly. I shouldn't be saying things like that about Jim's wife, but," she shook her head. Stray strands of hair that had come out of the clip fell over her eyes. "I just had to get that off my chest." She absentmindedly brushed at her hair. "I feel so sorry for him. He just lost his only brother, and his wife doesn't even care. She barely made it back to town in time for the funeral."

Drawing another calming breath, she continued on a new subject. "How is Drake coming with the investigation? It has to be hard for him to investigate his uncle's murder."

I gave her my standard answer on that subject. "Drake doesn't talk to me about the case. That wouldn't be very professional." If he knew I'd been asking questions at the bank, he would be upset with me. Since I hadn't asked about the missing funds, I wasn't sure what he would think I had done wrong.

My cell phone vibrated where it was clipped at my waist. Checking caller ID, I sighed, turning away from Linda. "Hello, Jane. What can I do for you?" I heard Linda's sniff of disgust.

"I was wondering if you could come over tonight. Jim has to work late at the store, *again*," she emphasized, "and I get so lonely out here all by myself." I was surprised by her request. This was her first attempt to be friends. Unless she wanted me to watch Hannah she hadn't wanted much to do with me.

"I'm sorry Jane, but I have plans with some friends." I'd piled up enough lies in one day to last a lifetime. I was glad I had an excuse, and didn't have to tell another one to get out of going out to the ranch.

June had called earlier about getting together for dinner with Jill. After witnessing that kiss between Drake and me the night before, I knew what they wanted to talk about. I'd have to be careful not to tell any lies over dinner.

"Oh. I guess we can make it another time." She sounded disappointed. Maybe I'd misjudged her, but something told me I hadn't. "I was hoping you could give me some advice about Jim. He's been so distracted lately. He won't accept the fact that Max was a crook, and now he's dead."

I bristled at her assumption that he was guilty. "Max was his brother. It's understandable that Jim would be upset. And we don't know that Max took the money."

"Oh, I know, but that's what it looks like. Anyway, that's not why I called. I just needed someone to talk to. Jim is always so busy with the store and town business. Now he's worried about that big store wanting to build here. He says it will ruin his business."

"If a big box store opens up in town, it will ruin a lot of small businesses."

"But it will be good for the town in so many ways. There's only that one grocery store in town."

"And that store will close along with Jim's store and

several others if a big store moves in. What will happen to all those families?"

"But that might be a good thing."

"Excuse me? You think ruining the livelihood of all those families would be a good thing?"

"Well, maybe not for everyone, but I think it would be good for us."

"How could that be good for you?"

"The store's going to go somewhere, why not Pine Mountain?" She didn't answer my question directly. "People are going to shop where they get the best prices." She gave a heavy sigh. "Look, that isn't why I called, I just thought you could come out to the ranch, and we could talk. I don't know what to do. Jim is taking all of this personally."

"How else is he supposed to take it? His brother was accused of embezzlement, and then was murdered. To me that means someone else took the money, and tried to frame Max. Now his livelihood is threatened. This is very personal." She was only thinking of herself in all of this, and didn't consider how it was affecting Jim or the rest of the town.

"Who would try to frame him?" Her voice quivered slightly.

"Look Jane. I really need to go. Like I said, I'm meeting friends, and I still have some work to do here at the library." Talking to her was like talking to a brick wall. She only heard what she wanted to hear.

"Oh, I thought you took the day off. That horrible woman said you weren't there when I came in this morning." She gave a weary sigh. "She's always so rude to me when I come in to see you. I don't know why she hates me." I could tell her she only came in to leave Hannah with me, but kept silent on that matter.

"I had some personal business to take care of first thing this morning. I've been playing catch up the rest of the day." My conscience pricked at me for the little white lie. As usual, Linda had kept things running smoothly while I was gone. I hoped God would forgive me once again.

Linda had tidied up the desk, and was working on the shelves when I was finally able to get away from Jane. It felt like she was up to something. She'd never shown any interest in being friends before today. Why the sudden desire now? Did this have anything to do with my visit to the bank, and my talk with Fred?

CHAPTER SEVEN

"Okay, let's have it." We had just been seated in the diner, and June was ready to start her interrogation. She had been patient long enough. "What happened after I saw the two of you in the parking lot?"

"Nothing happened." I hoped my face wasn't as red as it felt.

"You know perfectly well what she's talking about," Jill said, elbowing me in the ribs. "She caught you and Drake making out in the parking lot after the meeting last night. So give. What's going on with you two?"

"Nothing is going on. It was just a kiss."

"Don't try to pass it off as a brotherly kiss," June said. "That was an intense moment." They were tag teaming me.

"Nothing happened. I went home and..."

"And what?" they asked in unison.

"And Bill was sitting on my porch when I got there. He just about gave me a heart attack."

"Bill, as in Bill Cox?" June hooted. "Was Drake with you?"

"No, of course not. I don't know where he went after I left, but I assume he went home. His home," I added. "What difference does it make anyway?"

June swiped at her forehead as though wiping sweat off. "Shoo. That would have been something if he'd been with you. Those two have been at each other's throats since high school. They got in one hell of a fight in the school parking lot right after you left town."

"What? You never told me. What were they fighting about?"

June smirked. "You, of course." They both laughed, but I noticed a slight chill from Jill. I always suspected she had a crush on Bill, but it never went anywhere because he had a crush on me. She had never said anything about it during my earlier visits either. There were a lot of people keeping quiet about their feelings in this town. Maybe it was time to open up.

"Why would they fight about me?"

"Bill blamed Drake for you leaving. He said Drake drove you away."

I stared at them like they'd each grown another head. "That's nuts. I was fifteen. I had no say in the matter. No one drove me away. Mom and Jim got a divorce. That certainly wasn't Drake's fault. She just got tired of being married. You know how she was, how she is."

"Well, Bill didn't see it that way," June said. "He blamed Drake. He said if Drake hadn't teased you all the time your mom wouldn't have taken you and Tim away. I'm not sure he even cared about any of the other steps, just you and Tim." When Mom and Jim got married, she brought me and two of my half-brothers with her. Of course, when she left, they did too.

June shrugged. "Both of them were crazy about you, but you only had eyes for Drake. It looks like that hasn't changed any." She snickered. "That always drove Bill nuts. I think it still does."

After the way Bill acted the night before, I thought she was probably right. Was that why he didn't come to town very often? Was he avoiding Drake, not crowds? Mom's marriage to Jim lasted longer than any of her previous marriages. Because of that, I had always been close to Jim. That hadn't changed because of the divorce. During the ten years since Mom and Jim were divorced, I had been to visit several times before moving back to Pine Mountain.

While Drake was in the Air Force, Bill was around when I came to visit. Not so much since I've been back. If June and Jill were to be believed, Drake is the cause of that.

"Oh, brother. Why do they have to act like little boys?" I sighed.

"It's my turn now. Do either of you have a love life we can dissect tonight?" I sat back and crossed my arms over my chest. They both had had serious relationships in college that had died a slow death when they moved home. It's hard to move to a small town from the big city. Jobs are less plentiful, and less exciting. Like me, they were both single.

"Maybe if you'd cut Bill loose, someone else would have a chance with him," was June's cryptic comeback.

"Someone we know?" I asked. From the blush creeping up Jill's face I could guess who she was talking about. "So that's the way the wind blows." I chuckled.

I gave Jill a pointed look. "Maybe Bill would act differently if he knew how someone else felt about him."

"I don't know what you're talking about."

"Riiight," I drew out the word. "I think it's time for you to fess up and tell him how you feel." Her face was beet red. I turned to her twin. "What about you? Any love interest I should know about?"

June looked at her sister, and they both shrugged. "Okay, we'll let you off the hook for tonight. But you've been in love with Drake since you were ten. Isn't it time to do something about it?"

"I will if you will." I looked at Jill again.

She sighed. "Maybe."

I looked at June. "Anyone you'd like to tell me about?" I wasn't going to let her off the hook.

"Nope." The blush creeping over her cheeks told me otherwise. "I think we've chewed that topic 'til it got hard," she said before I could press the matter. I guess they didn't want to talk about their love lives, just mine. "What's up with Jane," she continued. "She spends as much time in Phoenix as she does here."

"Phoenix? What are you talking about? She just got back from visiting her mother in Denver."

"No," June shook her head. "I saw her in Phoenix a couple of weeks ago. She was with some guy, and they looked pretty chummy."

"When was that?"

She was silent for a minute, figuring back in time. "I guess it was about two weeks ago. What difference does it make? Who's the guy she was with?"

"That's a good question. Maybe I'll ask her sometime." It sounded like she might be having an affair.

"What's going on with the case?" They were through with that subject as well.

I shrugged. "Your guess is as good as mine. Drake doesn't discuss the case with me. He's made a point of telling me several times to stay out of things."

Jill giggled. "See, he's still got a thing for you."

"What thing?" I asked. "I'm not sure 'a thing' is something I want with a man."

"You know what I mean. He's still head over heels about you."

"If you think that's what it means when he says to stay out of his case, you're wrong. He even threatened to arrest me if I tried to mess with his case."

"He'd arrest you?" That wasn't what they expected me to say. But they weren't ready to drop that subject. "Well, if that's what it took to keep you safe from a murderer, I guess that makes sense."

It was late when I pulled into my driveway. Once again I'd forgotten to turn on the yard light when I left that morning. I put a motion sensor light on my mental shopping list. I surveyed the porch and side of the house for any shifting shadows. I'd had enough surprise visitors recently. I didn't want another one.

When all looked calm, I opened the car door, moving quickly to the house. Another item I needed on my shopping list was a dead bolt lock for both doors. If a credit card could bypass the current lock, it was time to upgrade.

It took a while before I could settle down and fall asleep. Were they right about Drake? Was he in love with me? My heart raced at the thought. He was the reason all men fell short in my mind. They simply didn't measure up. I wasn't sure he felt the same about me though. I finally fell into a restless sleep. When I woke up the following morning, I was as tired as I'd been when I went to bed. I was grateful it was Sunday. I didn't have to go to work.

Drake was standing outside the church when I arrived. My steps faltered slightly, but I managed to keep walking. "Good morning." His dark gaze swept over me, causing my heart to skip a beat. If he was in love with me as June and Jill said, why doesn't he come out and tell me, instead of playing games? "Rough night out with the girls?" He cocked one eyebrow.

"Are you keeping track of me?"

"I'm the chief of police. I have to have eyes and ears everywhere in case things get rowdy." He chuckled.

"So you have people spying on me." It was more of an accusation than a question.

"No, just making sure you don't get into trouble. If I remember correctly, the three of you managed to get into mischief when you were younger. Those two you were with last night still do, every now and then. I wouldn't be much of a police chief if I didn't keep an eye on the trouble makers."

Their assertion that he was in love with me still sent shivers up my spine. What was I supposed to do? I decided to play it cool. "Whatever. Are you coming inside, or did you come here to check up on me?"

"Oh, I'm coming in." As he reached for the door, his phone buzzed on his hip, stopping him. "Um, hold on a minute."

"Don't you know you're supposed to leave your cell phone at home when you come to church? The least you could do is turn it to vibrate."

Ignoring me, he pulled his phone off the clip on his belt. "Yeah, Cox here. What's up?" Turning away from me, he was all business. "Where? I'll be there in five." Replacing his phone, he turned back to me. "I have to go, Holly. Go inside, Dad's already here with Hannah."

"Just Hannah? What about Jane?"

"He didn't say. I really have to go. I'm sorry."

"What's going on, Drake? What happened?" I put my hand on his arm, hoping he'd stop long enough to tell me what happened.

"Police business, now go." He was impatient to leave, but he didn't want to go until I went inside. Dipping his head, he surprised me by placing a quick kiss on my lips. He pulled the door open, giving me a gentle shove inside. "I'll see you later."

Just that quick he moved down the steps. Watching from the doorway, my heart fluttered in my chest. He really was something else. He waited until he pulled out of the parking lot before turning on his lights and siren.

When I turned away from the door, I saw Jim visiting with friends. He was holding Hannah. When she saw me, she gave a squeal of delight. At least I hoped it was delight. She held out her pudgy little arms for me to take her. "Where'd Drake go?" Jim frowned as he relinquished his daughter to me.

I shrugged. "He got a call, and had to take off. Probably an accident." Something told me that wasn't the case. The last time there were police sirens I thought it was an accident as well. Instead, it was much worse. I hoped another body hadn't been found.

Throughout the service, I was distracted by my conversation with Jane the day before. Why would she think it would be good for her and Jim's marriage if he lost his business? Losing the hardware store would only make things worse for them. Granted, he would still have the ranch, but would he be able to support them on that income alone? I had no idea what his finances were like.

Even more disturbing was what I'd learned from June. Had Jane been in Phoenix, not Denver like she told Jim? Who was the man she'd been with? I didn't know what to think.

When Pastor Ned stood up for the benediction, once again guilt pricked at me. I'd zoned out for the entire message.

"Is everything okay?" Jim frowned at me when we were outside. "Your mind was somewhere else during the service. Did Drake say anything about what happened?"

"No," I shook my head. "I just have a lot on my mind. Is Jane all right?" She often begged off joining him for church. I didn't know what her excuse was this time.

"She said she wasn't feeling well enough to come to town." I could hear the doubt in his voice.

"I don't mean to pry, but is everything okay with the two of you?"

He heaved a sigh. "If it wasn't for this little gal," he looked down at his daughter, "I'd say I made a big mistake. I don't regret for a minute that she was born. I have three terrific sons, but Hannah fills me to bursting with joy every time she smiles at me." Anyone could see his love for her when he looked at her. She was playing with his bola tie now, trying to put the ends in her mouth.

I wondered what would happen to Hannah when one of them, or maybe both of them, decided they wanted out of the marriage. Jim would fight with everything he had to keep his daughter here. Jane not so much, I thought. I didn't doubt that she would use Hannah to get everything she could in a divorce. It was just a matter of time before one of them decided they'd had enough.

"Are you coming out to the ranch for lunch?" he changed the subject.

"Thanks, but not today. I have a few things I need to do to get ready for the week ahead." I was still looking for the "clues" Max said to follow. I didn't know how long he'd been in my house before I came home that night. If he'd left something there for me to find, I needed to keep looking.

The road leading to my small house was blocked with police cars and tape. It didn't take much of an imagination to figure out why Drake had been called away from church.

Unable to go any farther, I parked alongside the road, and waited for someone to come tell me what was going on. When the coroner's van came down the street, I bowed my head. *Please God, put a stop the evil that has taken over our town.*

I let out a startled shriek when someone tapped on my window. "Darn it, Bill," I whispered. This was getting to be a bad habit with him. My heart had nearly jumped out of my chest. Pushing open the car door, I stepped out to glare at him. "I wish you'd stop trying to give me a heart attack. What's going on? Who died?"

"Some young guy," he shrugged. "I don't know him. He might be a tourist." His face was white, and his hands were shaking.

"You saw the..." I couldn't finish my sentence.

He nodded gravely. "I found him. I was checking things out along the forest trail when I stumbled on his body. Literally, I almost fell on top of him."

"Oh, Bill, that must have been terrible. Do you know how he died?" I had my fingers crossed that whoever it was, he hadn't been murdered.

Gulping convulsively, he nodded his head. "Two bullet wounds to the chest, just like Uncle Max." I gasped, covering my mouth with my hand. "I called Drake. It doesn't look like you're going to be getting in your drive any time soon. You might want to go out to the ranch for a while."

"If you found him in the forest, why would that keep me from going home?" I had a bad feeling about what he was going to say next.

"The forest trail leads up to your place," he said. "I found him in the trees behind the shed in your yard."

The breath I'd been holding came out in a whoosh. "Oh, my gosh. What was a tourist doing out here?"

"The victim isn't a tourist." We both gave a startled jump when Drake spoke.

"Who is it?" Bill and I spoke at the same time.

"His name is Fred Brewster. He worked at the bank."

I gasped again, and my head began to spin. They each gripped an arm, easing me back onto the front seat of my car.

"Did you know him?" Drake asked the question, but I could see jealousy in Bill's eyes.

"No, well, I met him, but I didn't know him."

"When did you meet with him? What was the reason?" Drake's tone was official now. He was in full interrogation mode.

"I went there to ask about..." I paused. He wasn't going to like my answer.

"About," he prompted, one eyebrow lifted slightly.

"I wanted to know about having funds transferred into my account." I hoped that was generic enough that he wouldn't assume there was more I wasn't telling. I should have known better.

"Transferred in, or out? Why did you really go there, Holly?"

"Stop treating her like she's a suspect, Drake." Bill glared at his brother. "She hasn't done anything wrong."

Drake ignored him. "Why did you go to the bank?" he pressed. "I told you to stay out of my investigation."

"It isn't a crime to ask about having money transferred into her account," Bill continued to defend me. "You need to back off."

"No, you need to back off." Drake rounded on him. "This is a police matter. You both need to stop poking around in my case." His face was a cold mask. I barely recognized him.

Bill started to argue, but I stood up to stop him. "That's enough, both of you. Bill, you need to let Drake do his job."

"He's accusing you of something, and I'm not going to let him get away with that."

Drake started to speak, but my glare was enough to make him sputter to a stop for a change. "No, he's doing his job. I wanted to see what it takes to wire funds into and out of an account."

"Why? Are you expecting a wire transfer?" His tone was mild, but I knew there was steel behind it. "Or were you checking to see what you could find out about who transferred the funds from the town's accounts?"

Bill stiffened beside me, but he managed to stay silent.

"Okay, I was hoping to learn something. But I didn't ask anything about that. My account is at that bank so there's nothing wrong with me asking questions. I wanted to know what the procedure was to have funds wired in and out of a *personal* account." I stressed personal account.

"Who else knew you were there?"

"Beth Ann Rodgers," I sighed. "She introduced me to Fred." Both men groaned now. They knew her reputation for exaggerating the truth. By night fall it would be all over town that I'd been in to see Fred. By tomorrow at this time, she might even have me linked to his death.

"What was he doing in the forest?" I asked, hoping to change the subject. "He didn't strike me as the hiking type."

"He wasn't in the forest unless you call your back yard the forest. I can't let you go home just yet. Why don't you both go out to the ranch with Dad? I'll let you know when we finish with the crime scene."

A crime scene in my back yard, I shivered. "Had he been in my house?" I remembered how easy Max said it was to get past the locks on my door. I kept forgetting to ask Jim for a couple of dead bolt locks.

Drake shook his head causing a lock of sun bleached hair to fall across his forehead again. "It doesn't look like he was in your house. The techs are still going over the scene."

"Was he...killed here?"

"I can't say right now. I'll know more when the techs finish up here." Can't or won't, I wondered. "I'll call to let you know when you can get in your house." I wasn't sure I wanted to come back. Max's body was found behind the library where I work. Now a body was found behind my house. Was someone trying to implicate me in both murders? Or was this a warning of some kind? Who would know Max had come to see me, and that I went to see Fred?

Drake had only taken a couple of steps away from me

when Wally burst through the crowd that had begun to gather on the street. "Another murder?" He charged at me with clenched fists. "Until you came here, this was a peaceful town. Now look at it. You and Max were both a jinx on this town."

Before Drake could move, Bill took a swing at Wally connecting with his chin. "Holly didn't have anything to do with this, and Max wasn't a thief. He was a victim."

"I want him arrested for assault," Wally snarled from his position on the ground.

"From where I stand, he was defending someone from your attack," Drake drawled. "Get out of here before I arrest you."

"You can't arrest me," Wally sputtered, getting to his feet. "I haven't done anything wrong."

"I can and I will if you don't get out of here right now. If Bill hadn't stopped you, you would have hit Holly."

The air turned blue with Wally's curses, but he left. His big truck roared to life at the end of the street minutes later. There were enough spectators to attest to the fact that he would have attacked me.

Bill's chest was puffed up at Drake's defense of him. Hopefully this would be the start of a better relationship between them.

"Go out to the ranch with Bill, Holly," Drake said again. "I'll call when you can come home." It was just past noon, and he already sounded bone-weary.

CHAPTER EIGHT

Bill followed me out of town in his forest service truck. I didn't feel like answering any questions, but I knew there would be all sorts of questions when we got to the ranch.

Jim was surprised to see me when I entered the kitchen. "I didn't think you weren't coming out for lunch." He was cleaning Hannah up after feeding her.

The eleven-month-old was fiercely independent, wanting to do everything for herself. That meant a mess when she tried to feed herself. One of her favorite foods was Spaghetti O's. Her cute little face was covered with orange sauce now. She squirmed away from the wet cloth, wanting nothing to do with it.

Hannah's face lit up when she saw me, her gooey hands reaching out for me to pick her up. She jabbered away as though she was telling me something exciting. "Give me a minute before you touch her, Holly, or your nice blouse will be ruined." He turned around when Bill followed me inside. Dropping the cloth he'd been using on Hannah, he began to sway. "Where's Drake? Is he all right?"

"He's fine, Dad. He'll be out here as soon as he can." Jim was shaking so badly, Bill helped him into a chair before he fell down.

"Oh, thank God. Too many things have been going on lately. I don't think I can survive another loss. Tell me what happened."

No one had seen Jane enter the kitchen until she gasped when Bill told about finding the body of Fred Brewster. "Oh my God." She slowly lowered herself to the floor, putting her head between her knees. "How could something like this happen?" Her face was ghostly white.

"Did you know him?" Jim asked. The suspicion in his voice brought her around quickly.

"No, no, of course not, it's just so terrible that someone so young is dead." The tears sparkling in her eyes said that was a lie.

"No one said anything about him being young. How did you know that?"

"Oh, well." The wheels were turning in her head as she tried to think up an excuse. "In a small town, you know who everyone is even if you don't actually know them. I've probably seen him around." Her fingers were twined together to keep them from shaking.

Giving his head a shake, he turned his back on her. There was little doubt in my mind that she knew Fred Brewster more than simply seeing him in town. Was he the man June had seen her with in Phoenix? This might be the proverbial straw that broke the camel's back for Jim. "Where did you find him?" he asked his son.

"Behind the shed at Holly's," the words came out on a sigh.

Jim frowned at me. "What was he doing at your place? Did you know him?"

"I met him for the first time the other day. I don't know what he was doing at my place." Out of the corner of my eye, I watched Jane go back down the hall. Whatever was going on with her, I felt certain Fred meant something more than a passing acquaintance to her.

It was several hours before Drake showed up. His face was lined with worry. Bill got three beers out of the refrigerator, handing one to Drake and one to his dad. "Don't tell me you can't drink when you're on duty. You've put in enough hours today. Take a break."

For once Drake didn't argue. Twisting the cap off the bottle, he downed half of it in a single gulp. "It looks like he was killed somewhere else and dumped behind your place," he said before anyone could ask the question. He avoided looking at me. "He was shot, two gun shots to the chest just like Max. Ballistics will tell us whether it was the same gun. There was a gun on the ground beside to him."

"Suicide?" Jim frowned. "He shot himself in the chest?" It was a question.

"No. Either shot would have killed him, so he couldn't shoot himself a second time. Whoever shot him wanted the gun found." Drake drained the bottle, setting it down on the table. "Someone tried to remove the serial number, but the techs think they can still pull it up. If the gun's been registered, we'll know who it belonged to. Forensics will also check for prints." He gave a sigh. "I'm betting it's been wiped."

"Why would the killer leave the gun when it will be so easy to trace it?" I asked.

Drake shook his head. "Criminals aren't known for being smart."

"Or maybe he was trying to frame someone else," I said. "I still think Max was framed." Drake was too tired to argue the point.

After several moments of silence, he looked at me. "This happened just a short time after you visited him. What did you ask?"

"I've already told you. I wanted to know the process of wiring funds to and from my account."

"But you already knew that since you worked at a bank while you were in college. What did you hope to find out?" When I didn't have an answer, he continued. "He was killed right after your visit. This looks more like a warning than a coincidence. You need to stop snooping, and stay away from the investigation."

"I wasn't snooping. Okay, maybe a little," I conceded when he gave me that look cops get when questioning a suspect. "But how did anyone even know I'd been there unless Fred told someone? Don't you see this means he was involved with whoever took the money? Whoever he told about my visit is the one who killed both him and Max." I felt like I was preaching to the choir. Drake had to be aware of everything I said.

"Leave this alone, Holly, before you get hurt, or worse."

His voice was tight.

Jane had barricaded herself in the bedroom, and didn't reappear the rest of the day, leaving Jim to care for Hannah. He didn't seem to mind, or notice that she didn't bother coming out when Drake arrived. Their marriage was quickly falling apart.

~~~

"I can't believe you did that. How could you do that to him? He was helping us." She kept her voice low so no one could hear her.

"I didn't mean to do it. He got spooked by that librarian's questions. He was going to go to the police. He had to be stopped."

"Not like that!" She almost shrieked. "That's what you said about Max. Did you have to…"

"Don't say it. Don't even think it. He didn't give me a choice. There was nothing I could do. Things have gotten out of hand. I just wanted the money so we could be together. We need the money."

"I know," She sighed. Tears clogged her throat making it difficult to talk.

"You said no one would figure out what you were doing, and no one was going to get hurt."

"I know, but that was before. It was either them or me, us," he corrected."

"We have to get away. What's going to happen now?"

"I don't know. We have to go on as before. Honey, I love you, you know that. It's going to be okay. You have to believe that I would never do something like that unless it was absolutely necessary. As soon as we get our money, we'll go away"

"When is that going to be? What's the hold-up?"

He drew a shaky breath. "I don't know. It's complicated. Do you still love me?" He began to whine.

"You know I do. I'll always love you. I just don't' understand why you had to…"

"Don't say it," he repeated. "It was an accident, that's all it was, an accident."

"Are you sure no one can trace this back to you? What if they figure out where the money went? It's safe, right?"

"Of course it's safe. Don't you trust me?" He sounded hurt.

"Yes, you know I trust you. I'm just scared. What if she keeps poking around?"

He drew a shaky breath. He didn't even want to think about what would happen if she kept poking around in their business. The bodies were beginning to pile up. If another one showed up, there would really be hell to pay. "I don't know," he finally said.

Tears were streaming down her face when she hung up a few minutes later. This had gone all wrong. None of this was supposed to happen. It had sounded so simple at first. With a pile of money, they could go away together. No one would know they were behind this. But somehow Max had figured out what they were doing. What had he told Holly? How much did she know? Things were starting to unravel.

~~~

The news of the latest murder spread through town like a wildfire. I was only slightly surprised when Beth Ann called me that evening. "Did you hear about Fred?" Her voice rattled my ear drums it was so loud. "Someone killed that poor boy I introduced you to the other day. How could someone do that? Does Drake know who did this horrible thing?" She finally stopped to draw a breath.

"I'm sorry, Beth Ann. I don't know any more than you do. We'll have to wait until Drake finishes his investigation."

"First Max was murdered, now poor Fred. I'll bet there's a serial killer loose in our town." She wasn't listening to me. "Who's going to be next? What if you're next?"

"Why would you even think that?" My heart was in my throat now.

"Well, Max was your uncle, and now Fred is murdered

right after you came to see him. It can't be a coincidence. I've always heard that the police don't believe in coincidences. You need to be careful." That sounded like a warning, or a threat. For several long moments I zoned out as I thought about what she said.

When she finally ran out of steam, I managed to ask a question of my own. "Do his parents live in town?" I didn't recall anyone with the last name of Brewster, but I hadn't lived here long enough to know everyone. They could have moved here after I left.

"No, he's from Denver. That's where his mother lives. His parents are divorced." She gave me a complete rundown on his life. He was twenty-one, and had only worked at the bank a few months. He didn't know anyone when he moved here. After more useless information, I finally managed to hang up. If Drake wanted the scoop on anyone in town, he should talk to Beth Ann.

She said Fred was from Denver. Jane's mother lives in Denver. Was that the connection between them? Maybe I should do a little digging on Jim's latest wife. He'd kick my backside if he knew I was even thinking about that.

~~~

"How did this happen?" Things were going to hell, and he didn't know how to stop them.

"You know perfectly well how it happened. If he hadn't panicked when she came to see him, he'd still be breathing. You need to calm down." It was clearly a warning.

"None of this was supposed to happen," he argued.

"Well, it did happen, so get over it." Her sharp response sent chills up his spine. *"You should have thought of the consequences before you included Max in your little game."*

"I didn't have a choice." He sagged against the chair cushion. She was right, but there was nothing he could do about it now. He had to figure a way out without getting caught. Everything had been right on track until Max realized he was playing the game for real. He didn't think anyone

would notice the small discrepancies in the accounts. But Max noticed. Who would think someone with his shady background would suddenly develop a conscience?

He'd done his best to cover his tracks, but the man was smarter than he looked. Max wasn't the only smart one though. He looked at his companion giving another shiver. She had played all of them for fools, including Max. What was she going to do next?

"We need to figure out what Max told her." Her calm voice interrupted his troubled thoughts. "She has to know something or she wouldn't be poking around. Maybe you should have gotten rid of her instead of Fred."

"It was an accident. I told you that. He came at me." He had to get away, but he wouldn't leave without what was his. His life was like a snowball rolling down hill, and he didn't know how to stop it.

"Keep telling yourself that. Maybe you'll believe it. You might want to remember that you're in this for murder now."

He gulped air. "I didn't mean to do any of that," he whined. "Nothing like this ever happened before."

"Because it never went this far before," she said.

"You said you could control him."

"Don't even think about turning this around on me." Her voice held a hidden threat. "Now get a grip before you give yourself away. If Holly keeps poking around, she might come across something to prove Max hadn't done it. We need to find out what Max told her."

"Maybe we should leave now before that happens."

She shook her head, sending her hair whirling around her face like a tornado. "I'm not leaving while there is still the chance that Max left something behind that would point in my direction. I'm not going to spend the rest of my life looking over my shoulder" She gave him the evil eye. "You need to remember who is in charge now."

~~~

"You arrested your father?" I was in shock. News like that

couldn't be kept under wraps, not in a town the size of Pine Mountain. "How could you do that?" We were in Drake's office at the police station the day after Fred's body had been found behind my shed.

"I didn't arrest him." He sighed in frustration. "I brought him in for questioning. The gun belonged to him. Ballistics show it was used to kill both Max and Fred Brewster. What else could I do, Holly? I wouldn't be doing my job if I hadn't questioned him."

"So he isn't in jail?" I sank down in the chair in front of his desk feeling lightheaded with relief. "What did he have to say?" I was only slightly mollified.

He ran his fingers through his hair making it stand up in spikes. "He's always kept his guns locked up, I know that. Since Hannah was born, he's been even more careful. When Tim came to stay this past summer, they went to the practice range for target practice. When they came home, the guns went back in the locked cabinet. He hasn't had them out since."

"So someone stole it," I said with determination. "Was the lock on the cabinet broken?"

He shook his head. "Holly, I know how to do my job. I've checked everything. If someone took that gun, they were very good at picking the lock. Or they had the key."

"How many people know where that key is kept?" I continued pressing him with more questions, but I was just adding to his frustration.

"It isn't a secret where he keeps the key. Anyone he ever went hunting with could know where to find it. Other than Tim, there haven't been any visitors since Hannah was born. Jane said she was too tired taking care of the baby to play hostess." There was a trace of sarcasm in his voice.

"Huh," I snorted, but didn't put my thoughts into words. He was probably thinking along the same line.

When his office door exploded open, hitting the wall, we both jumped in surprise. "Where is he? What have you done to him? How could you do this to your own father?" Jane didn't stop for him to answer her questions. "How could you think he would do something like this? He would never hurt anyone."

"Simmer down, Jane. I didn't arrest Dad. I just had to ask him some questions."

"Oh." She didn't know what to say to that. She looked around sheepishly.

"Where's Hannah?" They didn't have live-in help. If Jane brought her along, had she left her in the car?

"What?" She acted like I was speaking a foreign language.

"Where's Hannah?" I repeated slowly.

"Oh, crap." Clapping her hand over her mouth, her eyes went wild. For several seconds she was too stunned to move. Then she rushed out of the office.

"Jane, where is she?" Drake called. We both hurried after her. Before we got outside, she was speeding down the street. "That damn woman." He slammed back inside. "Apparently she left the baby at home. Alone. She should never have had a baby. But since she did, she needs to take care of her."

I was torn between following Jane to make sure Hannah was okay, and staying here to find out more about the latest murder. The gun belonged to his dad. Who had access to the gun cabinet? I settled on the latter, and said a prayer that God would watch over Hannah and keep her safe.

"Did you find any fingerprints on the gun?"

"You know I can't discuss an ongoing investigation with you." He sank down in the chair behind his desk.

"I'm not a reporter. I'm not going to leak anything to the press." When he remained stubbornly silent, I pressed him with more questions. "Do you know of a motive for Fred's murder? He was so young. What could he have done that meant he should be killed?"

Another thought came to mind. "Did he have anything to do with that store coming here?" I was still trying to make a connection between everything that had happened lately. It seemed too much of a coincidence that the town's money went missing at the same time a big chain store was trying to make ground roads in town for them not to be connected.

"I don't see how he could have, but I'll be looking into that as well. *I'll* be checking," he reemphasized. "I want you to stay out of this." When I started to bristle, he held up his hand. Coming around his desk, he sat down on the corner, his eyes dark with emotion, searched my own. It felt like he was looking into my soul.

"Two people are already dead," he said softly. "I don't want that to happen to you." Reaching out, he pulled me out of the chair and into his arms. For several minutes his lips explored my face before settling on mine. When he lifted his head we were both breathing hard. This was what I'd wanted for so long. I didn't know if this was the right time for it though.

"Please stay out of this, Holly," his voice was a tender caress. "I can't keep you safe if you keep poking around."

"Do you think Fred was killed because I was asking questions?" That question had plagued me all night, giving me little rest. I felt responsible, but not threatened. "Does that mean he was involved?"

He sighed. "I don't know if he was involved. From what I gathered from the manager, he was a low level employee. He didn't have any authority. If he wasn't involved, maybe he had figured something out, and that's why he was killed."

"How well did Jane know him? She was pretty upset when she heard he'd been killed."

He shook his head causing that same lock of hair to fall over his eyes. He was past due for a haircut. "I've tried to stay out of Dad's marriage. I couldn't believe it when he said they were getting married. She's more glitz and glamor than jeans and cowboy boots. I do know she's tried to convince him to sell the ranch. It's too far out of town for her."

I gasped. "He wouldn't sell it, would he?" I loved the ranch. I couldn't imagine him selling it to please Jane.

"No, he'd never sell it," Drake said. He still had his hands on my waist, keeping in place. "The ranch has been in our family for four generations. My granddad had a pretty good grasp on finances. Both the store and the ranch are tied up in a trust. Max didn't want any part of either of them, but I don't think he would have agreed to sell." He heaved a sigh. "With Max gone, I'm not sure how that changes things. Max had no heirs, and no will. No matter what, Dad wouldn't sell."

"Who was involved with getting the store to build here?" I needed to move away from him, but couldn't find the initiative to do it. "Jim said Max was trying to stop it. Maybe that's why he was killed."

"Unfortunately, it's not that simple." He sighed. "Emails contacting the corporation about the store were found on the server. It was suggested that there could be big tax breaks if they brought the store here."

I gasped. "How could anyone make that kind of offer without the town council and mayor signing off on it? Who sent the emails?"

Drake sighed. "That's the problem. They were traced back to Max's computer. It looks like he wasn't trying to stop the store from building here. He was behind it in the first place." Whether he realized it or not, he was giving me information about the case.

I pulled away from Drake, taking a step back. "I don't believe that for a minute. Whatever was going on, Max was scared of something or someone. When he came to see me, he said he didn't take the money but it was his fault. What if he found out who was behind this store's attempt to build here, and wanted to stop it. Wouldn't the person behind this want to discredit him? They wouldn't want any opposition to their plans. Maybe they managed to embezzle the money, making it look like Max did it."

"You're seeing conspiracies where there aren't any. I've seen the paperwork. Max was trying to stop the store, but first he was trying to convince them to move here. The emails came from his computer," he stated again.

"So when he changed his mind, maybe that's why he was killed."

"Do you really believe that a major corporation would kill someone because he opposed them? That's a little farfetched even for your mystery-loving mind, don't you think?" He lifted one eyebrow.

"Maybe, but it isn't out of the realm of possibilities either." I stubbornly stuck to my theory. This was an argument we'd had several times since this began. I believed Max when he'd said he didn't take the money. I also believed he knew who did. I wish he'd confided in me. I had no idea what trail he told me to follow. Maybe I should go to that shack in the woods. That might be a good hiding place for any clues. How well had Bill searched it?

"I need to get to the library. If Wally finds out how many times I've been late recently, he'd try to get me fired." I tried to make a joke, but it was also the truth. Wally hated anyone connected to the Cox family. You'd think he let go of his grudge since Max was gone.

Entering the library through the back door, I took out my cell phone before going to my desk out front. "Hi Jane, how's Hannah?"

"She's fine of course." Her voice quivered slightly. "Why would you think otherwise?"

"You left her alone to come into town. Anything could have happened while you were gone." There was a note of accusation in my voice now.

"If you were so worried about her, why didn't you come to check on her? On second thought, I want you to stay away from Hannah. She's my baby, and I'll take care of her without your interference." She hung up before I could say anything.

That didn't work out so well, I thought. I didn't think her ban would last long though. Next time she needs a babysitter, she'd bring Hannah to me.

Drake showed up on my doorstep later that evening. "A peace offering." He held up a bottle of wine. "Mind if I come in?"

My stomach fluttered, but I stepped back allowing him in. After the kisses we'd shared in his office that morning, this might not be such a wise move. But it was time to find out if there was really something between us after all this time.

"A peace offering for what?" Getting two glasses out of the cabinet, I looked over my shoulder at him. "We can agree to disagree."

He poured a generous amount of wine in each glass before handing me one. "Things have gotten a little complicated between us lately. I want to make sure we're all right."

"Okay." My stomach fluttered again. I was unsure what he was hinting at. I decided to change the subject. "I've always heard if a case isn't solved within the first forty-eight hours it gets much tougher to solve."

"Tougher, yes," he nodded his head, "but not impossible. I will find out who killed Max and Fred and who stole the money."

"Don't forget that someone invited that big store to come to town. I don't believe Max did anything that people are accusing him of."

"Yeah," he sighed. "That's why the peace offering." He pulled out a file folder he had in his jacket. "These are copies of the documents Max signed with the corporation agreeing to let them build a big store here. There are also copies of transfer forms, wiring the money out of the town's accounts."

I grabbed the folder out of his hand. "I guess a peace offering was needed after all. Were you hoping to get me drunk before showing me these?"

"Holly, please understand. I have to look at the evidence. I can't let my emotions cloud the issues. Look at what I brought. It's pretty clear Max was involved."

I flipped through the papers, one by one. It was as he said; Max's signature was on each form. But something was off. Taking my time, I went through them again. Finally, a light came on in my mind.

"Do you see anything wrong with these signatures?" I handed him the transfer forms. A smug smile lifted the corners of my mouth.

"It's Max's signature. Holly, I don't want to believe he would do something like this any more than you do. But the proof is right in front of us."

"No, it's not. What you're calling proof against him, I say is proof of his innocence." Next I handed him the two sets of letters between the corporation and what is supposed to be the town's treasurer. "Check these out. Do you see any difference?"

A frown creased his forehead as he compared the signatures. Giving his head a shake, he looked at me. "What is it I'm supposed to see?"

I picked up a small tablet, handing it to him. "Sign your name five times," I instructed.

He frowned again, but did as I said. "Okay, now what?" He handed the tablet back to me.

"Do you see any differences between those signatures?" I tilted my head to one side.

"Sure, no one signs their name exactly the same each time." Even with Drake's scribbled signature, there were small differences.

"Take a look at those transfer forms again." He picked up the forms, studying them carefully. "Do you see any differences in the signatures?"

He studied the forms for a long moment, a frown drawing his brows together. Unlike so many men, Max had beautiful handwriting. He had been very precise. Even at that, there were small differences each time he signed his name. It was the same with everyone.

For several more minutes, Drake compared all of the signatures. "There is no difference in the letters on these transfer forms or the first letters to the corporation. It's like a stamp of his signature. These are copies of the originals, but I swear someone signed the forms I have in my office."

"Someone yes, but not Max," I agreed. "Someone else traced his signature to make it look like he authorized the transfers. If you'll check the letters between the town and the corporation building the store, you'll find the same thing. Someone else tried to make it look like Max was dealing with them. When he discovered what was happening, he tried to undo what had been done. That might be when the transfers were made. Someone was trying to frame Max."

"They did a damn good job of it, too." He gave me a quick hug. "Thank you. If you hadn't kept poking at me, I wouldn't have brought this out here to prove my point."

"Poking at you, huh? You mean like this?" I poked him in the chest with my finger.

"Yeah, like that." He grabbed my hand, pulling me against him as he fell back on the couch. I giggled when he started tickling me. Giving him a shove, we were in a full out wrestling match that quickly changed from playful to passionate. Somehow we'd rolled off the couch onto the floor without noticing. He was holding me down with his body, his dark eyes even darker as he looked down at me.

My breath caught in my throat as I waited for him to kiss me. But he didn't move. He stared at me with an expression I couldn't decipher. When it became too painful to wait any longer, I grabbed the front of his shirt pulling him to me. With his lips on mine, I felt like I was melting into him. He rolled over until I was on top of him, his strong arms locked around me.

Finally coming up for air, he rested his forehead against mine. "What am I going to do with you?"

"What do you want to do?" I wasn't sure what I expected him to say.

He gave a bark of laughter. "Maybe I'll show you someday. Until then…" His voice trailed off as he pulled me down until his lips rested against mine again. It was some time later when he finally pulled away from me. "I think that's enough for now." His voice was hoarse like he hadn't used it in a long time. "Dad would skin me alive if he thought I was playing fast and loose with you." He sat up.

"Are you?" I held my breath waiting for his answer.

"You should know better than that, Holly." He gave me another heart-stopping kiss. "It's taken you a long time to make your way back home. You have to know I'm not going to let you leave again." For several more minutes all was quiet in my little house.

Finally, he pulled back, clearing his throat. "Maybe I'd better leave."

"What? Aren't you even going to finish your glass of wine?" I held out his glass to him.

"You little tease." He chuckled, taking the glass, emptying it in one gulp. Gathering up his papers, he stood up. "Thanks again, Holly. I wouldn't have thought to compare the signatures with one I knew Max had written."

"Do you think that's why Max and Fred were killed?" I still had a lot of questions, least of all about us. Where was this going, whatever this was?

"I don't know anything for certain, but I'm going to keep digging." He was all business again. "Before I can do anything I have to get more than these signatures as proof Max was innocent. I'm not going to say anything to Dad right away, so you're going to need to keep this just between us."

I frowned at him. "Why don't you want to tell your dad? He needs to know Max wasn't a thief." Maybe he hadn't been talking about the case. That wasn't a comforting thought either. Why wouldn't he want his dad to know there might be something between us?

"If the guilty party thinks I've accepted the evidence he planted, he'll relax and mess up. When he does, I'll be right there to nab him. But you need to stop digging. Okay?" Assuming I would agree, he gave me one last kiss, and disappeared into the night.

CHAPTER NINE

I flopped back on the couch. My head was spinning with everything that had happened in a short time. I no longer had any doubts about my feelings for Drake. I was wholeheartedly in love with him. Picking up the glass of wine still on the table, I took a sip. He hadn't said as much, but if his actions were to be believed, he was also in love with me.

Bowing my head, I said a prayer. *Let this be real, Father God. I love him like life itself.*

One topic we failed to mention tonight was the gun found beside Fred Brewster's body. It belonged to Jim. How did it get beside the body? I didn't believe for a moment that Jim had killed anyone. He wouldn't have left a body behind my house either.

Drake said any number of people would know where the key to the gun cabinet was kept. If there hadn't been any visitors to the ranch since Hannah was born, that left Jane. What did that mean? I didn't care for the woman. Was that clouding my thoughts on the matter? Why would she kill someone and try to frame her husband?

It came back to money. Drake said she'd tried to get Jim to sell the ranch. If she didn't like living on a ranch or in a small town, why had she married him? Once again, it was the money. Jim wasn't wealthy, but he was far from destitute. After talking to June and Jill, I was convinced she was having an affair. Had her lover taken the gun, hoping to frame Jim? How did the missing money and the big store fit in with Jane having an affair?

I had thought about looking up Fred on social media, but forgot about doing it until now. If he and Jane were both from Denver, maybe I'd find something to connect them. But what good would that do? He was gone. What difference did it make now? My mind was spinning with all of these questions. I needed something to distract my thoughts.

Taking my Kindle, I headed for my bedroom. It was too early to go to sleep, but maybe I could get wrapped up in the latest cozy mystery I was reading. After reading the same paragraph for the third time, I set it aside. The questions kept swirling around in my mind.

Drake said the assistant treasurer had discovered the missing money when Max didn't come to work that morning. Why would he start looking into the accounts simply because Max didn't show up for work? If he'd been worried about Max, why not call the police or Jim instead of looking at the accounts?

I didn't know if he was a local, or a transplant like Fred Brewster and me. Had he been hoping for the job of treasurer when Jim gave the job to Max? Maybe it was time to check out Jack Johnston. Max had gotten the job of Treasurer instead of Jack. Was he the kind to hold a grudge, like Wally had for years? Did he even want the job?

Why had Fred Brewster been killed right after I talked to him? Had he been involved with the embezzlement? I was certain he'd known Jane, but how well did he know her?

These were all questions to ask Drake, but for now I needed to keep a low profile. If he thought I was interfering in his case, he'd lock me up and throw away the key.

Picking up my tablet from the bedside table, I signed onto the internet. I'd searched the town's website looking for something, anything, to help me figure out who had taken the money. I'd come up blank every time. It had been a while since I logged onto Facebook. Maybe I would find something there.

If Fred Brewster had an account, someone had already deleted it. Another dead end, I thought, frustration eating at me. Next I tried Jack Johnston only to come up blank. Either he didn't have a Facebook page, or I couldn't match his profile with a man I didn't know.

Logging out of my account, I set the tablet back on the night stand. It was time to get some sleep. Only two more days before the Thanksgiving break. The kids and teachers alike were anxious for the four-day-break. The library would be the last place any of them would go. Maybe during the lull, I could do a little more checking. Something had to click soon.

~~~

As expected, the following day was uneventful. Considering all that had been going on, I looked on that as a blessing. I even managed to do a little snooping on the computer but without any success. I hadn't seen Drake, but I was hoping he would come over again.

It was after five-thirty when I pulled into the driveway at my house. Daylight had turned to dusk. For once I'd remembered to turn on the porch light before I left home that morning. Reaching out to put my key in the lock, the door swung open. Someone had been in my house, or they were still in there.

Anger overrode common sense. Grabbing the only thing at hand I could use as a weapon, I headed inside. Swinging the broomstick like a sword, I hit everything hard enough to make noise without breaking it. I wanted to make as much noise as possible. If the burglar was still inside, he'd know I was coming.

Halfway through the house, I realized what a stupid move this was. I should have called Drake immediately instead of going in. Giving a mental shrug, I continued down the hall. Since I was this far through the house, I might as well keep going. The closet door in my bedroom was open a crack.

As I stepped into the room, the closet door exploded open. Dressed in a black hoodie with the hood pulled low enough so I couldn't see his face, the intruder knocked me down. I got one good whack in with the broomstick. He gave a grunt of pain, but didn't stop. The back door slammed and he was gone.

"That'll show you not to mess with me," I shouted. "I hope I gave you a good bruise. Too bad something isn't broken." As the adrenalin seeped out of my blood stream, I began to shake hard enough that it was difficult to hit the numbers on my cell phone.

"Hey there, beautiful."

"Someone was in my house." I cut in, not giving him a chance to say anything else.

"Don't go in there. I'm on my way." Before he disconnected, I heard his big SUV roar to life. He must have been outside when I called.

"Too late," I said, but he didn't hear me. He was going to be mad at me when he got here.

I was waiting outside minutes later when he pulled in behind my car. Pulling me into his arms, he simply held me for several minutes. I could feel his heart was pounding against mine.

Drawing back, he looked down at me. "Are you okay?"

Here goes, I thought. "Yes, but someone is going to have a sore leg for a few days." I waited for the explosion that didn't come.

"You were in the house when you called me." It wasn't a question. I nodded my head, and he sighed.

"Why did you go in if there was the chance someone was still in there?"

I bristled at his tone. "Haven't you ever done something only to realize later it was a stupid move? I was angry that someone broke into my house." I sighed. "I was also angry at myself. When Max came here, he told me I needed to get new locks. Anyone could get in with a credit card. I kept forgetting to ask your dad. I won't forget again," I muttered.

"You're sure no one is in there now?"

I nodded. "He's gone. He was hiding in my closet. I did manage to hit him before he got away."

"With what?" He didn't release me as we headed for the back door. I pointed at the broom I'd propped beside the door. He shook his head. "You're a feisty one, that's for sure." He chuckled, and I breathed a sigh of relief. I'd weathered that storm.

We did a walkthrough to see if anything was missing. My

television was still in the living room where it belonged. The few pieces of jewelry that were precious to me were still in their hiding place. I kept a small amount of cash for emergencies, but it was still in the drawer. My laptop was propped up beside the couch. I didn't know if it had been touched. Even my tablet was where I'd left it the night before.

"Nothing is missing. What was he looking for?" I was puzzled. "Is this connected to the murders?"

"Maybe you got home before he could take anything." He pulled me against his hard chest, looking down at me. "Don't ever go in a building when the thief might still be there. He could have killed you." A shudder shook him at those words.

"Did you get a look at the intruder?" he asked. I'd started a pot of coffee, and was peering into the refrigerator to find something I could fix for dinner.

"No," I spoke without looking up. "He had on a hoodie. It happened so fast that's all I saw."

"Was he tall, short, thin, fat?" he pressed.

"From my vantage point on the floor, he looked pretty tall. But he could have been average height."

"What were you doing on the floor?" He turned me around so I was facing him. "Did he hit you?" His hands moved up and down my arms looking for any injuries.

"He knocked me down when he burst out of the closet. It knocked the breath out of me, that's all. That's when I managed to swing the broom at him. I caught him on the ankle. He's going to have a pretty good bruise on his leg." I was proud that I'd been able to do that much.

"You keep saying him. Are you sure it was a man?"

I thought about that for a few minutes, finally nodding my head. "Yeah, I'm pretty sure it was a man. I think," I added softly, not so sure all of a sudden.

"What are you looking for? Do you keep money in there? That's the first place a burglar will look."

I was looking in the refrigerator again. "No money, just food, and not much of that either." I sighed. "I haven't been to the grocery store since that night I fixed steaks for us. Cooking for one is harder than cooking for a big party." Dinner for one usually consisted of a sandwich, or a cup of soup. Breakfast was yogurt with fruit and granola.

"Why didn't you say so? Put some clothes in a suitcase and let's get out of here. We'll go to the diner."

"Why do I need to put clothes in a suitcase to go to the diner?" I frowned at him.

"I'll put new locks on the doors tomorrow. Until then, you can't stay here."

"And where do you think I'm going to stay?" I braced my hands on my hips.

"You can stay at my place."

"Oh, the gossips would have a field day with that." I immediately thought of Beth Ann. She'd have us married with two kids by the end of next week with that piece of gossip.

"I don't care what the gossips say. You can't stay here without better locks on the doors. You need window locks as well. Come on, I'm hungry." He headed for my bedroom. I guess he was going to help me pack.

"Not so fast." I grabbed his arm. "I'm not going anywhere, especially not your place. This is my home, and some punk isn't going to chase me out of it."

"Come on, Holly, be reasonable. There have been two murders in town."

"And neither of them involved burglary."

"You don't know whether this break-in was the run-of-the-mill burglary, or if it was somehow tied in with what's going on in town. I'm not taking chances with your life."

My stomach churned uncomfortably, but I stubbornly stood my ground. "I'm not staying at your place, Drake. This is a small town. Everyone would know about it before daybreak."

"As long as we know we haven't done anything wrong, what other people think doesn't matter."

"That's just like a man," I snapped, standing my ground.

"No one cares if a man sleeps around, but a woman's reputation is ruined by the same actions."

Seeing that he wasn't getting anywhere with his argument, he gave a frustrated sigh. "Okay, if you won't stay at my place, I'll take you out to the ranch. You can stay there until..." He stopped talking when I shook my head.

"I'm not going anywhere."

Sitting down on the couch, he gave a little bounce. "Well, this doesn't feel too bad. I guess I can bunk here for one night." He continued when I started to object. "Your closest neighbor is too far away to know or care whether you have company all night or not. I'm not leaving you alone tonight."

Frustrated, but also happy, I turned back to the refrigerator to hide my smile. He cared enough about me to not sully my reputation. Pulling out bread, cheese, butter and milk, I spoke with my back to him. "I'm going to have a grilled cheese sandwich and tomato soup. If that sounds good to you, I'm willing to share."

"Feisty and stubborn," he grumbled. He didn't have any room to complain, I thought. He was just as stubborn.

Coming up behind me, he wrapped his arms around my waist. "Just the qualities I love in my woman," he whispered as he nuzzled my neck. Goosebumps moved up my arms as a shiver shook me.

"If you think this is going to make me change my mind, you're wrong." There was no heat in my voice now.

He chuckled, but continued to nibble at my neck, moving to my earlobe before turning me in his arms. His lips claimed mine. For a long while, we forgot all about food.

~~~

He'd gotten out of her place by the skin of his teeth. He held a cold compress to the bruise just above his ankle. It was already turning purple. It hurt to put weight on that leg. Maybe she cracked a bone. Going to the doctor was out of the question though. He couldn't very well explain how he got the bruise. For a small gal she sure could pack a wallop?

There hadn't been time to find anything before she showed up. He couldn't decide if it was a good thing he'd left the door unlocked or not. It made for a fast getaway, but he hadn't known she was in the house with him until she started making enough noise to wake the dead.

Max had warned him that he wasn't going to get away with this, that he'd left evidence of what he'd been doing. "He taunted me," *he said in the empty room.* "He said this was his last con. What the hell is that even supposed to mean?"

Those had been the last things Max said before he pulled the trigger. He hadn't even realized he'd pulled it until Max dropped to the ground. He'd probably given whatever evidence he claimed to have to that stupid librarian. If that wasn't the case, where was it? If he'd given it to his brother or nephew, the money would be back in the town's accounts, and they would be in jail. He had to find it, and soon, or his own life might be in jeopardy.

CHAPTER TEN

Jim hosted a big party every Thanksgiving, but after Max was murdered he had canceled it this year. The gathering would be much smaller with only a few friends and family attending. With two funerals only days before Thanksgiving, and the town's money still missing, few people felt much like celebrating, especially Jim. The threat of the big box store moving in had people arguing over what would be best for the town.

The small mom and pop stores would all be boarded up, and the downtown would be deserted. Even those in favor of the big store coming here didn't want to see that happen.

Mona, Drake's and Bill's mother, had always shared the holidays with the family when I'd been living here. It wasn't any different now. Unfortunately, Jane objected to Mona having anything to do with the family.

People were gathered in the great room when I arrived with my dish for the potluck dinner. Propane heaters had been set up on the patio in case anyone wanted to go outside. All conversation in the great room stopped at the sound of Jane's screeching voice coming from the kitchen. "Why does *she* have to be here? She doesn't belong here."

For a moment I thought she was talking about me. I was still persona non grata as far as she was concerned because I had questioned her about leaving Hannah alone. I couldn't help but eavesdrop. My feet were rooted to the spot, and her voice was loud enough to carry across the room.

"Keep your voice down. She'll hear you." Jim always tried to keep the peace, but it wasn't working this time.

"Good, maybe she'll leave. I'm tired of her popping in anytime she wants. You'd think this was still her house the way she just takes over every time she's here."

"She doesn't 'pop in', and she might not feel it was necessary to take over if you'd do something around here." I'd never heard Jim talk to her like that before. Maybe he was getting tired of the way she treated everyone, him included. "She will always be welcome in my home."

"This is my home, too. Either you tell her to leave, or I will."

"You'll do no such thing. She is still Drake's and Bill's mother."

"That may be so, but she isn't Hannah's mother. I am. She has no business being here to celebrate Hannah's birthday. I want her gone."

Hannah's first birthday was two days away. Jim had decided to celebrate her birthday along with Thanksgiving. Probably not a good idea, I thought.

"I think everyone has heard enough for one day, don't you, Jane?" Drake had entered the kitchen from the outside door.

"Shut up, Drake. This is none of your business. You're as bossy as your mother. This is my house, not yours."

"This will always be home to all of my children. You need to settle down." At the crack of a hand hitting flesh, I jerked back. I wasn't sure what Drake would do next. I didn't know about the others, but I'd heard enough.

I was still holding my dish of Crispy Cheesy Potatoes. Turning away to find somewhere to put it, I nearly bumped in to Mona. "Oh, um, hello, Mona." Taking a step back, I looked at the closed kitchen door. It was embarrassing being caught eavesdropping, but I wasn't the only one. She and everyone else had heard the argument, and I felt bad for her.

She could be a bit overbearing at times, but unlike Jane, she was never vicious. When Mom and Jim were married, Mom never objected when she visited. They had even become good friends after Mom and Jim split up. Because Mona had never remarried, I always wondered if she regretted her divorce.

"What should I do with this?" I held up my casserole.

She shrugged. "You'll have to wait until her highness is finished chewing Jim a new one to ask her. Far be it from me to come in here and take over." She gave a husky chuckle. It didn't sound as though she was upset by what she'd overheard. "Until they're finished in there, I guess you can place it on the table.

"It looks like Jim has his hands full with that one," she continued, nodding towards the kitchen. "I think I could use a glass of wine. Care to join me?"

"It's a little early for me, but I could use a cup of coffee." I followed her over to the bar where several bottles of wine were sitting out. A large coffee urn was on the bar as well.

"I wasn't surprised when you moved back to Pine Mountain after college," Mona said, a teasing smile playing around her lips. "You always loved this little town. Of course, this is where Drake is now as well." I could feel my face heating up. I didn't know how to respond to that comment, so I didn't say anything. She hadn't disapproved of my crush on her son when I was younger. It didn't appear she would object now either.

"How's your mother?" She changed the subject. "I heard through mutual friends that she got married again. I hope she picked more wisely this time. She hasn't had much luck so far." From someone else it would sound like a dig, but she didn't mean it that way. She was simply stating facts.

"She's fine. They're living in Florida right now. I'm hoping she will finally settle down. Ted's a nice guy."

"Her other husbands were as well." She shrugged. "But I understand where she was coming from. Sometimes it's simply too hard to choose one from all the fish in the sea." She chuckled at her own joke. Maybe I'd mistaken her choice to remain single as wanting Jim back when she really wanted to play the field.

"Hi, Mom." I jumped when Bill came up behind me. My nerves were still on edge. He placed a kiss on her cheek before turning to me. This was the first time I'd seen him since the night he kissed me. I took a step back to avoid a repeat.

"Hi Bill. How are you?" My voice was a little stilted, but

there was nothing I could do about that. I wasn't going to encourage him. I didn't know if he'd told Drake about finding where Max had been hiding in the forest. Was that where he left the clues he'd mentioned? If that wasn't the case I had no idea where to look.

"Hi Mom, Bill." I gave another start when Drake joined our little group. Like Bill had, he placed a kiss on his mother's soft cheek. Draping his arm around my shoulders, he pulled me to his side in a possessive gesture. Or was I reading more into it than he meant? I wasn't any better at deciphering the hints or clues he was giving than I was at finding anything Max left behind.

Bill's shoulders stiffened and his fists clenched. I wasn't sure what he was planning when he took a menacing step towards his brother. Placing her hand on Bill's arm, Mona shook her head at him. "Relax, Son. Everything always works out the way it's supposed to." It was a rather cryptic remark, but I didn't ask her to clarify.

"Is everything okay in there?" Mona asked Drake, looking towards the now silent kitchen.

"For now," Drake shrugged. "Maybe she's dealing with post-partum depression, or something." Hannah was almost a year old. It was a little late for that to kick in. Jane simply wanted everything her way, and tended to throw a temper tantrum when that didn't happen.

Bill looked between his brother and his mother. "What'd I miss? What's she done now?" He'd missed the fireworks between his dad and Jane.

Mona shrugged. "Her usual complaint. She doesn't want me here."

"Can't she get it through her head that you have a right to be here? You're our mother."

"Your father has always been gracious, and let me share in all of the holidays with you both. Maybe I'm pushing it with this one though." Mona lifted her shoulders in a fatalistic shrug. It must be hard for her. Because she never remarried

Drake and Bill were all she had.

Jim came out of the kitchen, stopping all conversation on that subject. The red imprint of Jane's hand was still visible on his cheek. "Hi boys, I'm glad you're here. Mona," he nodded at his ex-wife. He bent down to place a kiss on my cheek. "Thanks for coming, Holly."

"I wouldn't miss it." An awkward silence settled over us for several long moments. He had to know everyone had heard what Jane said. He was embarrassed by that as much as anything else.

He turned to his oldest son. "Have you found out who…" It wasn't necessary for him to finish his sentence.

"I'm still looking into things, Dad. I'll let you know when I find something out."

"What's taking you so long?" Bill snapped. "I'd bet my next paycheck that Max didn't steal that money. Whoever did is obviously the killer. How hard is it to figure that out?" He turned to look at his dad. "Who took the gun from the gun cabinet?" It almost sounded like an accusation. He kept his voice down, but the others in the room were straining to hear what was being said.

If no one else had been in the house but Jim and Jane, that narrowed the suspect pool. My bet was on Jane, but I couldn't see her shooting someone, much less two people. She wouldn't want to get her hands dirty. It would also take someone much bigger than she is to move two bodies.

"Enough!" Jim snapped. "I don't need any more problems today."

Bill frowned. He wanted to ask more questions, but didn't want to upset his dad further. "I'll explain later, dear." Mona linked her arm through his. "Come on. Buy me another drink." She held up her empty wine glass. He obediently allowed her to lead him to the bar. Looking over her shoulder at Drake, Mona gave him a wink. Or was she winking at Jim? You just never knew what Mona was up to.

"Are you all right, Jim?" I moved out from under Drake's

arm to give Jim a hug.

"I will be. Don't worry. I'll see you later." He wandered aimlessly around the room, greeting the few guests gathered there.

"Where's Jane?" I whispered once Jim stepped away from us.

"Since she's acting like a two-year-old who didn't get her own way, maybe Dad sent her to her room." He tried to make light of what happened in the kitchen. Dipping his head, he placed a soft kiss on my lips causing my heart to bump in my chest. I knew how I felt about him, but his feelings towards me were still a little murky.

"I don't think this is something we should be doing here," I whispered once I was able to catch my breath.

"Why's that?"

"People might see us. I don't want anyone to get the wrong impression."

He frowned at me. "What wrong impression is that?"

"Well, you know what I mean."

"No I don't. Does it embarrass you to be seen with me?"

"That's not it, and you know it."

"You don't want anyone to know you're my girl?"

"Your girl?" I looked up at him through my lashes. My heart was beating a wild tattoo in my chest. "Isn't that something we should discuss?"

"I thought we'd said all that was needed saying the other night. Did I read things wrong?" He tilted his head to one side. Mischief danced in his eyes.

"I don't remember a lot of words being said that night. Silent communication doesn't work so well. Maybe next time you could try talking."

He'd been the school heart throb all through high school. According to June and Jill, that hadn't changed any. They had filled me in on the number of women he'd gone through since he moved back home. I didn't want to be another notch on his bed post.

He chuckled, placing another kiss on my lips. "When this shindig is over, maybe we can go back to your place for a little more discussing. How does that sound?"

I was saved from answering when Jim called everyone into the dining room. Gathered around the big table, he said grace, giving thanks for all that we had. Jane didn't bother to put in an appearance after their fight. She'd probably gone somewhere to sulk.

When she finally came out of hiding, she didn't bother with food. She sat at the bar like it was her throne, glaring at anyone who spoke to Mona. As soon as her glass was emptied, she refilled it. She was going to be drunk before the day was over. Several times I caught a glimpse of a man talking to her, but I didn't know who he was. Maybe he was the man June had seen her with in Phoenix. It took a lot of nerve to invite your lover to your home while your husband was there. How would I find out who he was?

A drunken hostess and a family fight were bad enough, but when Wally stumbled in ready to rumble people parted like the Red Sea. "The town is broke but the mayor holds a party. You got something to celebrate, Mr. Mayor?" He was weaving, barely able to stand up straight. "I don't know why I thought it would be any different. Maybe the town's footing the bill for this shindig. Did you help that worthless brother of yours steal our money?" When he made his way across the room, there was blood in his eye.

"Go home and sleep it off, Wally." Drake intercepted him before he reached Jim.

Wally unsuccessfully tried to shake off Drake's grip on his arm. "What home? If yer damn uncle hadn't stolen my girl, I'd have a home, maybe even some kids." He was beginning to blubber. How long was he going to live in that dream and on that grudge? Whoever the 'girl' was, she had moved on with her life a long time ago. It was time for him to do the same. "Max took her, now I don't have anyone." He leaned against Drake's shoulder, wiping his damp eyes.

Drake pulled his cell phone off his belt, calling for a squad car. As drunk as Wally was, it was a miracle he hadn't crashed before he got here. Drake wasn't going to let him drive home.

Two officers arrived a few minutes later. I recognized Officer Babcock from the crime scene behind the library. The second officer was several years older than Babcock. I'd seen him around town, but I didn't know him. "See to it that he gets home in one piece," Drake instructed quietly. "Just drop him on the couch, and leave. You don't need to stick around. Hide his keys so he can't drive until he sobers up." Drake was doing the man a favor by not arresting him. I didn't think Wally would remember this in the morning. He probably wouldn't appreciate it either.

With that settled, Drake pulled me aside. He wasn't finished with what he was now calling 'our discussion'. The high pitched wails of a baby could be heard down the hall putting an end to his plans. Hannah wasn't happy about being ignored, and was letting everyone know she was ready to get up from her nap.

Looking around for Jane, I found her across the room talking with the same tall, handsome man I'd seen her with earlier. Once again she was holding a glass of wine. Either she didn't hear her daughter's cries, or chose to ignore her. "What do you think she'll do if I go get Hannah?" I looked up at Drake.

"As long as you change her diaper, she'll be fine with it. She's the poorest excuse for a mother I've seen in a long time." He followed me down the hall to Hannah's room.

Her tears dried up quickly once she saw us coming to her rescue. She reached out her chubby arms to be picked up. "Do you want to join the fun, Sweet Thing?" I kissed her cheek as I lifted her out of the crib. "Let's get your diaper changed and go find your daddy."

She jabbered happily throughout the process. Once that was finished, she wanted down. At two days shy of one year old, she was walking everywhere. I wondered how Jane was going to keep track of her, or would she even try?

We each held her hand, and made our way through the people standing around. I didn't see Jane or the man she'd been talking with. I didn't even try to locate her. By this time she would be too drunk to hold her daughter.

Mona intercepted us as we made our way across the room to Jim. "Well, hello there, cutie." She bent down to Hannah's level. "Will you let me hold you?" She held out her hands.

Hannah had no problem with Mona holding her, and went willingly into her arms. Maybe Hannah was simply so starved for attention from her mom that she was willing to let anyone love on her.

"What the hell do you think you're doing?" Jane's screech came from the open patio door. "Get your filthy hands off my daughter!"

Everyone froze as Jane stumbled across the room. She was obviously drunk, and in no shape to hold a wiggling baby. But that didn't stop her from trying. She snatched Hannah out of Mona's arms before anyone could stop her. Frightened by Jane's loud voice and being jerked away from Mona, Hannah let out a loud howl.

In the process of whirling away from Mona, Jane lost her balance. Bill managed to keep her from going down, and Drake caught Hannah. By this time, the baby was in full-blown hysterics.

Jim came in from the kitchen in time to see Bill holding Jane up, and Drake taking Hannah out of her mother's arms. "What the hell's going on in here?" He looked around, hoping for an explanation.

"Dada." Hannah hiccupped, holding out her arms for him to take her. Big tears ran down her cheeks.

"That bitch was trying to take my baby!" Jerking her arm away from Bill, Jane pointed a finger at Mona. She staggered slightly at the sudden move.

"What?" Jim looked between his ex-wife and his current one.

"I told you to get rid of her. Now maybe you'll believe me." Her words were slurred, and she weaved unsteadily as she confronted her husband. Bill didn't try to steady her. If she fell, she fell. "She was trying to steal my baby."

"You're drunk." Jim didn't bother to keep his voice down. "Go somewhere and sleep it off." He turned away from her.

"I think it's time for me to leave," Mona whispered. She turned away, but not before I saw tears swimming in her eyes. Her sons started to follow her outside, but I stopped them.

"Let me do this." Taking my spare key off my key ring, I hurried after her. "Wait up, Mona." I held the key out to her. "It's too late to go anywhere. You know where I live. Stay with me for the night."

"That's sweet of you, but not necessary. I have a room in town. I'm not silly enough to think I could stay here. That would be pushing things. Jane has made it clear on many occasions that she doesn't want me around. She'd probably slit my throat in the night." She gave a humorless laugh, and placed a kiss on my cheek. "I'll see you later." She looked so sad. My heart broke for her.

I started to turn away when I heard her speak to someone. "Everett? What are you doing here?" His deep-toned voice drifted to me on the wind, but I couldn't hear the words. It was getting dark, and I couldn't see his face very well. Obviously she knew him, but what was he doing out here?

"Mona, are you all right?" I took a step towards them. My heart was in my throat now.

"I'm fine, Holly. Go back inside. It's cold out here." I could hear them talking as he followed her to her car. He opened the door for her, then turned away. *Keep her safe, Father. We've had enough trouble lately."*

As he stepped under the yard light, I caught a glimpse of his face. The fleeting look pricked my memory, but I couldn't place where I'd seen him before.

CHAPTER ELEVEN

It was still early when I went back inside, but people were ready to call it a day. The last confrontation was the final straw. Everyone was pitching in to help clean up the trash, everyone but Jane, that is. I didn't see her anywhere. Maybe she'd taken Jim's words to heart and gone to bed. I didn't see the man she'd been with either.

"Is Mona okay?" Jim had his hands full of plastic cups, plates and silverware.

"Yes, I think she'll be fine." I wished I could say that for certain. Who was the man she walked off with? I hadn't been able to get a clear look at his face in the semi-darkness, but I was certain I'd seen him before.

"I'm glad Hannah is too little to remember this," he sighed. "We didn't even get to cut her birthday cake." A lock of hair had fallen across his forehead, and he gave his head a toss to put it back in place. The gesture was so like the one I'd seen his oldest son do many times, causing me to smile.

"You can still have a small party just for the family on her big day," I suggested. Looking around, I didn't see Hannah or Jane. "Where is she?" I mentally crossed my fingers, saying a prayer that she wasn't with Jane.

"A couple of the girls took her in the other room to distract her. As for her mother, I don't know and don't care." His broad shoulders slumped in defeat. "I never should have had this dinner party. Not with everything that's been going on." Giving a weary sigh, he shook his head. "I don't know what I was thinking." I wasn't sure if he was talking about the party or his marriage.

Jane wasn't helping clean up, but that wasn't unusual. Even sober, she wouldn't pitch in. The queen of the castle didn't do hard labor. I was being snarky, but I couldn't seem to help myself after the way she'd acted earlier.

Bill and Drake were across the room having a serious

conversation. Neither of them looked very happy with the other one. I could only guess at the topic. At least they weren't going to add to the drama by making a public display with a fist fight.

When the last of the guests were gone, it was time for me to leave. The house had been put back in order, so Jim wouldn't have to worry about that in the morning. If only it was that easy to fix the mess his marriage had become, I thought. I prayed that when the time came, Jane wouldn't use Hannah as a pawn against Jim. That happened too often in a divorce.

Saying my good-byes to Jim, I picked up my casserole dish. Jane still hadn't put in an appearance. Even if she was standing next to me, I wasn't sure I could be civil. She had put on quite the display. Like Max's funeral, this Thanksgiving would be talked about for years. Drake followed me outside. "Would you like some company tonight?" He leaned down, placing a soft kiss on my lips.

My heart fluttered. "Um, I don't think that's a good idea. This is a small town, and you and your dad are public figures. The town gossips would chew us up if you spent the night at my house again."

"Well, that wasn't what I was suggesting, but if you're offering." He chuckled softly.

My face felt like it was on fire again. Mom always said I had 'hoof and mouth disease'. I'd certainly put my foot in it this time.

"No, but I thought…Never mind. I need to go home." I clicked the key fob to unlock the car door. With my back to him, he wrapped his arms around my waist nuzzling my neck. Goosebumps moved up my spine. When I didn't resist, he turned me in his arms, his mouth descending on mine.

"Now can I come over for a little while?" he asked, in a hoarse voice.

"I, um," I had to clear my throat before I could get any words out. "I guess it would be all right if you came over for a little while," I stressed, hoping he would stick to that time frame. Besides, I wanted to know what he and Bill had been discussing when I came inside.

During the short drive from the ranch to my small house at the edge of town, I tried to talk myself down off the emotional cliff I was perched on. I needed to clarify my position in his life before this went any further.

The door had barely closed behind us when Drake pulled me into his arms. Somehow we made it across the room, falling on the couch without any mishap. It was several long minutes before either of us spoke.

"Can we just talk for a minute?" I pushed on his hard chest. I needed some space in order to gather my wits about me. We were both breathless. I stood up to put some distance between us. My legs felt like Jell-O, and I wasn't sure they'd hold me up for very long.

"Okay. What is it you want to talk about?" He stretched his arms out along the back of the couch, completely at ease.

I was suddenly nervous. How could I phrase my questions without sounding like a complete idiot? "Um, did you mean what you said earlier?" I stammered.

He stood up taking several steps towards me. I backed up an equal number. My mind turned to mush when he got too close, making it impossible to think straight. I needed to keep a clear head, or I'd never figure out whether we were on the same page regarding where this was heading.

My house was small, and eventually I backed into the wall stopping my retreat. Within arm's reach, he pulled me to him, but he didn't try to kiss me. "I said you are my girl. If that isn't clear enough for you, I'll put it another way. It's been a number of years since we spent any quality time together. I want to do that, before I make my formal proposal."

"Proposal," I interrupted, my voice nothing more than a squeak.

"Yes, my proposal," he chuckled. "If you have any lingering doubts about my intentions, let me put them to rest. I fell in love with a knobby kneed girl of ten, and time hasn't changed that. Except for the knobby knees," he qualified with a chuckle. "We still need to get to know the adult us before we can go any further. Have I been clear enough?"

My heart was pounding so loud in my chest, I was sure he could hear it. Since I couldn't make my voice work at the moment, my head bobbed up and down. Again there were several long moments of silence before either of us spoke.

We had made our way back to the couch. This time, Drake stood up, stepping away from me. I wasn't the only one who needed some space in order to maintain a clear head.

"What were you and Bill discussing when I came back inside? It looked pretty serious." A change of topic might help cool things down a little. "Neither of you looked very happy."

"Yeah, I guess we both had reason to be upset. He's been keeping a few things from me." He narrowed his eyes at me. "I guess you have too. Why did you tell him to go looking for where Max had been hiding? Why didn't you come to me with that?"

"What would you have said if I told you to look in the forest for his hiding spot?" I asked. "You were so intent on keeping me out of your investigation you wouldn't have listened to me. I told you he was dirty and hadn't shaved in a while. That means he wasn't staying in a motel. You saw how he looked when you found his..." I stopped, taking a deep breath before I could begin again. "When you found him," I finally finished. "Besides, Bill knows the forest better than you do since that's where he works. It was logical that he'd be able to find where Max had been hiding faster than you could. Did he tell you what he'd found?"

Flopping back down on the couch, he drew a calming breath. "Yeah, but it turned out to be nothing. I'm surprised that old shack is still standing. A good wind would knock it over. He said it looked like someone had been staying there, but the only thing in the shack is an old chair we'd taken out there as kids. He said that's why he didn't come to me with it."

"You don't think he'd hold back something he found if it implicated Max in the embezzlement, do you?"

He shook his head, sending that lock of hair over his forehead. This time, I didn't resist the temptation. I combed my fingers through his thick mane to put it back in place. Taking my hand, he placed a kiss in the palm and curled my fingers over it.

Drawing a shaky breath, he answered my question. "He knows better than doing something like that. The truth would come out eventually, making it look pretty bad for him. He loves his job, and wouldn't do anything to jeopardize it."

"So you still don't know who was behind the embezzling, or who killed Max." There was disappointment in my voice. "Why was Fred killed? He really didn't tell me anything. I didn't ask him about what happened to the town's money. I just wanted to know how a wire transfer was done."

"But you already knew the answer. Didn't you work at a bank while you were in college?"

I tilted my head to look at him. "How did you know that? We weren't in contact at that time." He'd commented on that once before.

"You told Dad and Mom. They kept me informed."

"They didn't do the same for me," I stated indignantly. "All they said about you was that you joined the Air Force. I thought maybe you'd become a pilot or something." We'd gotten off topic again.

"No, police work was always where I planned on going. I think you knew that at one point."

He was right. It had always been his dream to become a policeman. How could I have forgotten that?

"What else were the two of you discussing?" I wanted to get back on track. "What was Bill upset about?"

"He wanted to know if my intentions towards you were honorable." I sputtered at that, but he ignored me. "He didn't like my answer. Seems he's been holding out hopes of his own.

I told him it was time for him to find his own girl. I was in love with you."

"You told him that before you told me?" I sat up straight.

"I didn't think it was necessary to put it into words," he chuckled.

"Oh. How did he take that?"

"For a minute I thought he was going to take a swing at me. Instead, he shook my hand, and said the better man won. I told him not the better man, just the right one for you."

"You're pretty sure of yourself, aren't you?"

He pulled me against his chest, his lips claiming mine in a heart-stopping kiss. When he lifted his head, he looked into my eyes. "Now tell me that isn't the truth."

I couldn't lie. He is and always has been the right man for me. I fleetingly thought that Bill gave up easily. His interest in me probably had more to do with the rivalry between him and Drake than it did me. Maybe now he would notice Jill was in love with him.

It was long past midnight when he finally left. We both had jobs to go to in a few short hours. I hoped we'd get this 'knowing the adult us' part over with soon so he could get on with the formal proposal.

~~~

The day after Thanksgiving is a slow day at any library. That's especially true in Pine Mountain. The students are out for a long weekend. They weren't worrying about term papers. Their parents were at all of the Black Friday sales in town or other towns around.

When the door opened, I was surprised to see Jane waltz in. She was wearing a pair of dark sunglasses that she didn't bother taking off when she came inside. She was probably nursing a hangover this morning.

"This town is so full of hypocrites," Jane snarled, as she came up to my desk. She was wearing the same clothes she'd had on the night before. Maybe she hadn't spent the night at home. I didn't want to go there.

"Really? What makes you say that?" At the moment she was one of my least favorite people. Hannah wasn't with her, and I hoped she hadn't forgotten about her baby again.

"No one wants that big box store here because it might hurt the local stores. But they'll drive fifty miles to shop at one. They just don't want it in their town." She looked around at the empty tables and book aisles. "That money could just as easily stay right here if they weren't such a bunch of phonies."

"It isn't the once a year sales that keep the stores here open," I argued. "It's the day to day buying that people rely on. If that store opened up here, the local stores wouldn't be able to match the prices. They would end up going out of business. The downtown area would become a ghost town."

"And such a wonderful downtown it is, too," she sneered. "It would be such a shame to see it change, even though it would be an improvement. I hate this town and everyone in it. I have half a mind to leave. I'd take half of everything Jim has. See how he'd like that." I noticed she didn't mention taking Hannah with her.

When Linda gasped, Jane turned to glare at her. In the silent library, Jane's voice had probably been heard even in the upper deck. "I'm not going to do that, so you can just put your hopes back in the box. He's *my* husband. If he wanted an old woman, he wouldn't have gone looking for someone young enough to be his daughter." She whirled around, stalking out of the library.

"She is such a witch," Linda whispered. "She'd stay married to Jim simply to punish him." There was nothing I could say to that. She was right. If Jane thought Jim wanted a divorce, she was vindictive enough to refuse to give him one, even if it meant she would be unhappy as well.

Worried that Jane had left Hannah alone at the ranch again, I picked up the phone. "Cox Hardware, this is Tom. How may I help you?" One of Jim's employees answered. Not everyone had driven fifty miles to the big box store. All of the local stores had sales going this weekend as well, including the hardware store.

"Hi, this is Holly. Can I talk to Jim for a minute?" I drummed my fingers on the desk, waiting for Jim to pick up.

"Holly, is something wrong?" He sounded worried. "I saw Jane's car pull out of the library parking lot. What did she have to say for herself?"

"Where's Hannah? She wasn't with Jane." I was beginning to panic when I heard the sweet cooing in the background. "You have Hannah with you." The words came out on a sigh.

"Yeah, and she's a great little sales lady. I should have thought about bringing her to the store before this. Everyone who comes in here wants to play with her. They don't leave without buying something either, even if it's something they don't really need." He chuckled.

Growing serious again, he asked, "What was she doing at the library? I doubt that she's read a book in the whole time we've been married." His voice was bitter. "I'm surprised she crawled out of whatever hole she had fallen into last night even though it's past noon."

"She wanted me to know what a bunch of hypocrites we all are since so many people are shopping at the big stores out of town today." A thought occurred to me. "Do you think she could be behind the store coming here?" I whispered, afraid to state the question aloud.

"I wouldn't put anything past her." He sighed. "I really can't talk right now. In spite of what Jane thinks, not all the people have left town to shop elsewhere. Things are hopping here. Thanks for checking on Hannah. I wouldn't leave her home alone, or in Jane's care." The line went dead. Had my assumption that Jane had spent the night elsewhere been correct?

NEVER CON A CON MAN
CHAPTER TWELVE

Jane had been gone less than forty-five minutes when she stormed back in. If she'd been out to the ranch and back, she had broken all the speed laws between here and there. She had a wild look in her eyes now. "Where is she? What did you do with her?"

"What are you talking about?" I stood up so she wasn't looming over me.

"You know damn well what I'm talking about. If you don't have her, that bitch does. Where did she take my baby?"

"Calm down. Hannah is with Jim at the hardware store."

"Huh? What's she doing at the hardware store?" Her anger evaporated, and now she seemed confused. She looked around to see who else had heard her outburst. Linda and I were the only ones in the building. Not even the book club women had come in today. They were probably out shopping.

"Someone had to take care of her. He couldn't very well leave her home alone, could he? If you'd been home when Jim left this morning, you would have known where Hannah was. Where were you last night?" I was taking a stab at the truth.

"That's none of your damn business." She turned on her spiked heels and stormed out again. Linda shook her head, but kept her thoughts to herself. I wouldn't mind being a fly on the wall at the hardware store if she was silly enough to go over there. I didn't think Jim would turn Hannah over to her.

On slow days like this, Linda and I spent a lot of time straightening the shelves and catching up on paperwork. Since the library was run by the city, not the school, we had to abide by the hours set up by the town council.

By mid-afternoon we were both bored. We'd done our best to avoid talking about what happened the previous day. She hadn't been at the ranch, but I was sure she'd heard from those who had been.

Given what June had said, and what I witnessed the day

before, I was fairly certain Jane was having an affair. If she spent the night away from home, Jim probably suspected as much as well. What he was going to do about it though was a mystery. This divorce would end up nothing like the one with my mom and her many husbands. Jane would try to take everything he owned and then some.

When Mona stopped in, she looked well rested and happy. I didn't know if the man she'd met at the ranch had followed her back to her hotel. I didn't want to be nosy and ask either.

"I'm heading home today, and I wanted to tell you goodbye before I left." This surprised me. She usually stayed the entire weekend. Guessing my thoughts, she added, "I have a couple of big clients I need to meet with first thing Monday morning. I still have things to prepare for the meetings." Mona owned an interior design business, and dealt with high-end clients.

"I'm sorry we didn't have much time to visit. Maybe we'll have more time at Christmas."

"About that," she hesitated. "I think I'll skip the fun this year. It will be different when my sons give me some grandchildren to play with." She lifted one eyebrow at me. I could feel my face heating up. It was clear that she wouldn't mind if Drake and I got together. If what Drake hinted at the night before, she might get that wish someday soon after all.

Sadness settled over me when she left. My own mom was on the other side of the country. I missed her more than I wanted to admit. While I was growing up, we'd been close. But she'd always been looking for something, or someone else, in her life. Hopefully, she would realize it wasn't another man she needed. Maybe Ted would help her to find the One that would fill the void for her. I wanted her to finally be happy.

An hour before closing Drake pushed open the front door. "Is there somewhere we can talk?" He stopped in front of my desk. From his serious expression I figured this was about police work, not us.

I spread my hands out to indicate the entire building. "I

guess this will do just fine."

When the meaning of my words sunk in, he took in the fact that the library was empty. "Where's Linda?"

"I sent her home a few minutes ago. There was no sense in both of us sitting here with nothing to do."

A slow smile spread across his rugged face. "We're alone?"

"We are." I nodded. "What can I do for you?" I stayed behind my desk to avoid temptation, but it didn't do any good.

With predatory precision, he moved around my desk, a teasing smile on his lips. Pulling me out of the chair, he wrapped his arms around my waist crushing me against his hard chest. After several heart-stopping kisses, he let me sit back down. I was disappointed and grateful it didn't go any further, all at the same time.

Seated in the chair across from me, he grew serious again. "I just came from the hardware store. Did you know Dad has Hannah over there? Why isn't Jane taking care of her?"

I shrugged. "You need to ask your dad that question. I don't think he trusts her with Hannah right now." I paused for a moment before going on. "She probably didn't spend the night at home. When she was in a while ago, she was wearing the same clothes she had on at dinner."

He shook his head, a look of disgust on his handsome face. "Was she sober?"

"I think so, maybe a little hung over." I shrugged.

"Why did she come here? She never appeared the least bit interested in reading a magazine, let alone a book."

"She actually came in twice. The first time she wanted to tell me what a bunch of hypocrites we all are." I explained about her little tirade against everyone who went shopping at the mega store in the next town. "I don't know if she is behind bringing that store here, but I do know she isn't against it. The second time she was looking for Hannah. If she didn't spend the night at home, what did she think Jim would do with her?" I tried to frame my next question without sounding nosy. "Do you think he'll divorce her?"

"That's anyone guess. He keeps his thoughts about their marriage private. If she's sleeping around, I hope he does something." He gave a hearty sigh, changing the subject. "How much longer before you can close up shop? It doesn't look like you're going to get a last minute rush to check out a book or look up something for a research paper."

Looking up at the big clock over the door, I sighed. "I still have a half hour before I can lock the doors."

"What's stopping you from closing early? I'm off duty tonight. Can I talk you into dinner at The Steak House?" It was the one fancy restaurant in town. If you can call a western motif fancy, that is.

"The one time I closed early is the one time Wally or some of his friends would be checking on me. I don't want to give him something else to complain about."

"I doubt that he has many friends left. He's managed to alienate nearly everyone in town. If he's not careful, he'll lose his business."

"I wonder how he's feeling today. He was pretty drunk when he showed up at the ranch yesterday."

Drake gave a dry chuckle. "Babcock said he slept all the way to his house. That was a good thing. At least he didn't puke in the patrol car. It took both of them to get him inside. He probably doesn't even remember being at the ranch. If he hadn't carried his grudge all these years, he could have a family by now. But it's easier to blame someone else for your troubles than claiming responsibility for your own actions." He shook his head.

He looked up at the clock again. We'd managed to kill another ten minutes. "I don't think anyone is going to complain if you close a few minutes early. Come on." He pulled me out of my chair again. "I'm hungry."

I made one last round of the stacks to make sure someone hadn't come in when I wasn't looking. It hadn't happened before, but I wasn't taking any chances. I didn't want to lock someone in overnight.

Only a few tables were occupied when we arrived at the restaurant a short time later. Until there was enough snow on the slopes to open the ski lodge, things would be slow in town.

"Hi, Drake." The hostess smiled seductively at him as she escorted us to a table. "Can I get you something to drink?" She made a point of ignoring me. I guessed her to be about my age. I'd seen her around town, but I hadn't met her.

"Just two coffees right now, Wanda. Thanks." Disappointed, she sashayed off.

I wish I had that swing on my back porch, the refrain from middle school popped into my head. "A recent conquest?" I asked, lifting one eyebrow. I tried to keep the cattiness out of my voice, but it was hard with June and Jill's tales of his dating habits filling my mind.

"Just a friend," he dismissed her actions as business as usual, and picked up the menu. The green-eyed monster had a grip on me. As though reading my troubled thoughts, Drake reached across the table to take my hand. "Nothing ever happened between us. She might have wanted it to, but I didn't." He raised my hand to his lips, placing a kiss in my palm.

Taking a deep breath, I tried to slow my heart rate down. He continued to hold my hand as we looked over the menu. After giving our order to the waiter, we fell silent for a few minutes. He played with my fingers, and the teasing smile on his face said he knew the effect he was having on me.

Looking around the restaurant, I searched for a safe subject. "This is a nice place. If memory serves, there was a different restaurant here when I was a teenager. How long has it been here?" During my other visits over the years, I had only gone to the diner.

"Yeah, there have been several different ones here. I think this one will last longer than some of the others. Bill and Susan moved here from California about three years ago. They wanted a quiet life, but Pine Mountain was completely alien to them." He chuckled at the memory. "They were like fish out of water for a while, but they've managed to assimilate into the way of life around here just fine.

"They tried their hand at winemaking before they opened this place. So far it's been a hit. The food's good, and the wine is not too bad either. Wanda is their daughter. She moved here with them, but goes back to California every few months. Pine Mountain is a little too tame for her."

Another silence stretched out. This 'getting to know the adult us' was more difficult than I expected. We knew each other, but there was still a lot we didn't know. I wasn't sure what questions I should be asking.

Wanda led a single man to a nearby table, drawing my attention. When she flirted with him as well, I decided that she flirted with all the men. Maybe she hoped she'd get a good tip or something. The man looked familiar, but I couldn't recall where I'd seen him before. "Do you know who that is?" I whispered, nodding at the man.

Drake looked over at him, giving a shrug. "No. Should I?"

"I don't know." I frowned. "He looks familiar."

"He's probably a tourist. If he lived here, I'd recognize him. I might not be on a first name basis with everyone in town, but I do know most of them by sight."

My gaze kept wandering over to where he sat. I couldn't get over the feeling that I'd seen him somewhere before. I spend most of my time at the library. That isn't a place tourists frequent. Going over the places I'd been recently, the memory remained just out of my grasp. When realization hit me a few minutes later, I gasped. "He was at the ranch last night," I whispered.

"What are you talking about?"

"That man, he was at the ranch. He met your mom as she was leaving. I think they know each other."

"Okay," he shrugged. "She's a big girl. Maybe she had a date after dinner last night." He didn't seem worried about it.

"But she wasn't expecting to leave so early," I argued,

looking over at the man again. "I've seen him somewhere else." I was thinking out loud, trying to remember what other place I'd seen him. I gave a startled jump when Drake took my hand again.

"Don't worry about it. It wouldn't be the first time Mom brought a friend up with her when she visits, a male friend," he qualified. "Maybe they had agreed to meet after the dinner. When things started to fall apart she might have texted him. It's no big deal." He turned his attention back to playing with my fingers.

That didn't explain the fact that he was at the ranch. "Why would he be at the ranch if he was meeting her in town?"

"What are you getting at?" A frown drew his eyebrows together.

"I don't know," I admitted. "I've seen him some place other than the ranch. I just can't remember where."

We were almost finished with our meal when my memory kicked in. I reached for Drake's hand across the table. "I know where else I saw him." My voice was barely above a whisper. I didn't want the man to know we were talking about him.

"What? Are you still talking about that guy?" He had already dismissed the man from his mind.

"Yes," I sent a cautious glance in the direction of the other table.

"Okay, I'll bite. Where did you see him?" His lips curved up in a teasing smile.

"Never mind." I resented his patronizing tone. Pulling my hand from his, I crossed my arms over my chest stubbornly.

"Oh, come on. Don't be that way. Tell me where you saw him."

After a moment I gave in. It was important for him to know. "That day I talked to Fred Brewster," I started. When his eyes darkened, I rushed on before he could say anything, "Wally was arguing with a man in the lobby when I was leaving, that man," I emphasized.

"Wally argues with everyone," he interrupted. "You know

that. He was probably drunk."

"Will you let me finish?" I frowned at him, and he held up his hands in a gesture of surrender. "Wally was talking about that big store coming to town. He got right in the man's face. I thought he was going to attack the guy. The manager had to come out and break things up. I think he works for the company trying to build that big store here." I related what I'd overheard. It wasn't much, but more than we'd had seconds ago.

"So you think the man Mom met last night is working for this corporation. Are you saying she's involved with this deal somehow? Why would she have anything to do with that? She doesn't even live here."

"That's not what I said. I'm just saying he met her outside as she was leaving. Did you know she went back to Phoenix today?"

"Yeah, she told me Wednesday when she first got to town. She has a big job coming up. What are you accusing her of?"

"I'm not accusing her of anything. I'm just telling you what I saw. That's the man Wally was arguing with, and I'm almost positive he's the man Mona met as she was leaving the ranch."

"Almost positive being the operative words here," he said. "I still don't understand where you're going with this."

I huffed, but didn't say anything for several seconds. With a heavy sigh, I shook my head. "I'm not sure what I'm getting at either." I leaned back in my chair. "Don't you think it's odd that the man working to get that store here was at your dad's ranch, and he met your mom as she was leaving?"

"Now you're accusing both of my parents of being in cahoots with that corporation." His temper was beginning to heat up right along with mine. "You're not even sure he's the same man who met Mom. It was getting dark when she left. Did you get a good look at his face?"

"Not exactly." I admitted. I was frustrated now. "If he is the same man, what was he doing skulking around in the dark?

I think she was surprised to see him there. Has your dad been able to stop them from opening a store in town? Have you found out who initiated the contact with them?"

"Every mayor and town council for the past twenty or more years has made an effort to keep big chain stores and restaurants out. That's why this thing with the big box store came as a complete surprise. If they finally got the approval to build with a bunch of tax breaks, that would bring in more chain stores. It would kill a lot of the smaller businesses." I noticed that he didn't answer my last question. The only chains in town were the hotels. Without them there wouldn't be anywhere for the tourists to stay during peak seasons.

Small town America was a dying breed, I thought sadly. An entire way of life would disappear if things continued the way they were going. Some people, Mona included, hated living in a small town. That didn't give anyone the right to ruin it for the rest of us. Not everyone enjoyed big city life. Still, I didn't think she would do something like that.

When the man finished his dinner, he stood up, coming over to our table. He held out his hand for Drake to shake. "Hello, Chief Cox." He nodded his head at me. "My name is Ernest Fletcher. I work for Dynamic Corporation." I frowned. That wasn't what Mona had called him.

Drake reluctantly shook the proffered hand. "What can I do for you?"

Without waiting for an invitation, Mr. Fletcher pulled up a chair and sat down. "I'd like a chance to discuss my company's proposal to build a store in town."

"I'm not the one you should be talking to."

"Maybe not, but you do have the ear of the mayor." He chuckled, like he'd just made a joke. "He's your father." Did he think Drake needed to be reminded of the connection he had with the mayor? "Maybe you could put in a good word for me."

"I know who my father is, but I'm not putting in a good word for you. I don't want your store here anymore than he does. In fact, very few people want your store here. It would put a lot of people out of work."

"Those same people, along with a lot of others, could find jobs in our store. Think about how many people one of our stores employs."

"Those people would go from owning their own businesses to being a minor employee of a big corporation. I'm sure those jobs pay minimum wage. That wouldn't be a good bargain for those folks. How many mom-and-pop stores have closed because your store moved into a small town? I'm sorry, but I'm not going to help you. Now I think this conversation is over. Unless you'd like to explain what you were doing at my father's ranch yesterday." I was surprised he brought that up. I didn't think he believed me.

"Oh, um, well," he stammered. "I'd heard your father had a party every year. I thought it would be a good time to meet some of the more influential people in town."

"It wasn't a party. It was dinner with family and friends. Maybe you haven't heard that my uncle was murdered recently. We weren't exactly in the mood for a party."

"Um, yes, I have heard about that trouble. I'm sorry for your loss," he added belatedly.

"My uncle was also the one trying to stop your company from building here. Quite the coincidence about the timing of his murder and your visit, don't you think?"

"What are you suggesting?" Mr. Fletcher sat back in his chair.

"Nothing," Drake said mildly. "Just stating facts. Were you hoping to dig up some dirt on people in the hope of forcing them to sign onto your little deal? Is this how big business works?"

"Certainly not." He sounded indignant now. "Besides, your uncle contacted our company in the first place. Not the other way around."

"I don't believe that," I said. Drake's expression clearly said he wanted me to stay out of this.

"Were you hoping to sweet-talk my mother into helping you convince Dad to sign on to your deal?" Drake continued like I hadn't interrupted. "I wonder what your company headquarters would think of your methods."

"Your mother? I don't know who you're referring to." His eyes shifted away from Drake as he spoke putting the lie to his words.

"Mona Gardener is my mother. I have it on good authority that you met her outside Dad's house when she was leaving."

"Oh, I wasn't aware she was your mother." Once again he couldn't look Drake in the face.

"Really?" Drake's brows rose slightly.

"Um, ah, yes," he stammered. "We bumped into each other at dinner Wednesday evening. We're staying at the same hotel. I asked if she was here for Thanksgiving. She happened to mention that she was going to dinner at her ex-husband's house."

"She doesn't usually make a point of telling people that he's the mayor. That's something you already knew.

Mr. Fletcher's face turned a slight shade of pink at that. "All right, I knew who her ex-husband was. That just means I've done my homework."

"You knew her ex-husband is the mayor, but you didn't know she was my mom? Either your research wasn't very thorough, or you just lied to me. I don't like it when people lie to me. It makes me wonder what they're trying to hide." Once again, Mr. Fletcher's face flushed, this time from anger. "Were you hoping to use her to crash my dad's dinner?" Drake was giving the man a hard time. I would hate to be a suspect in his custody. He was relentless.

"I wouldn't put it quite like that."

"Did she know why you were in town?"

"I told her I work for a large corporation, if that's what you mean."

"But you didn't tell her you were trying to build one of your big stores here."

"I don't discuss business with strangers."

"But you don't have a problem with trying to gather information about those strangers, and using it to your advantage."

"It wasn't like that. Your mother and I enjoyed a few drinks in the hotel lounge, and went our separate ways. She said she was leaving town today. I haven't seen her since."

"You still haven't explained what you were doing at the ranch after dark." Drake circled back around to that topic. "How did you explain to her what you were doing there?"

"Look, I haven't done anything wrong." He avoided answering Drake's question.

"Maybe not legally, but I'd say your ethics leave something to be desired. As I said before, this conversation is over."

Fletcher looked like he was going to argue further when I spoke up. "What did you say your name is?" Both men looked at me like I'd lost my mind.

"Ernest Fletcher, why?" He turned back to Drake, dismissing me as a minor irritant.

"Is that the name you gave Mona when you met her?" I wasn't finished with him yet.

"I don't know what you're getting at." His face took on a greenish tint when he realized his mistake. Bluffing wasn't his strong suite.

"Because when she saw you last night, she called you Everett. That's close, but not the same. Did you give her a phony name so she wouldn't know what you were really doing in town?"

"You must be mistaken." Without another word he stood up, marching out of the restaurant. He kept his head high, and his back ridged.

"Your intimidation skills are impressive," I complimented Drake when we were alone again.

"I gotta say you aren't so bad yourself," he admitted. "That certainly threw him off his game. I think it's time I had a little chat with someone from Dynamic Corporation."

"Do you think he is capable of killing someone if they stand in his way of closing a deal?"

He shook his head. "No, he's short on business ethics, but I don't think he'd kill anyone. Hopefully, we've seen the last of him and Dynamic Corporation. There are enough other towns willing to allow them to build a store there."

I wondered if meeting Mona in the bar that first night was as accidental as he claimed. It was quite a coincidence that they were staying in the same hotel. If he had researched Jim and others in town, it wouldn't be hard for him to know who Mona was. She is very active on all forms of social media. He could have found out she was coming up here, and hoped to use her to talk with Jim.

CHAPTER THIRTEEN

He was still nursing a sore ankle, thanks to that damned librarian. He refused to say her name. What he wouldn't give to pay her back in kind. His hands itched at the thought of getting them on her. She was causing him all sorts of trouble, and he didn't think that would end any time soon.

Someone had been snooping on the town's web site recently. Pine Mountain wasn't a tourist destination in the off seasons. Until it started to snow in earnest, few people were checking out the town.

Since that first town hall meeting though, there had been a big uptick in web site hits. Someone was checking things out; things that ordinary tourists had no interest in. If he had to venture a guess, that damned librarian was snooping around. He should have stopped Max before he went to see her. She was going to ruin everything if she didn't let up. He wasn't going to let a librarian outsmart him.

~~~

For six months I'd managed to avoid Beth Ann. With the missing money, Max's murder, and then Fred's murder following my visit, I was her new best friend. She seemed to think I should be a fount of information. Telling her anything was like e-mailing the entire world.

The library had only been open a few minutes Saturday morning when she pushed through the door. She sat down in the chair in front of my desk, an expectant smile on her face.

"Did you have a nice Thanksgiving?" Her loud voice echoed in the cavernous room. I got the feeling she already knew all about what happened. There had been enough people at the ranch willing to pass along any gossip. She probably knew more about what happened than I did, plus some things that hadn't happened.

"Yes, it was very nice. How was yours?"

"Oh, um, mine was nice, as well." She wasn't here to talk

about herself. She was looking for dirt on others. "Kind of quiet," she added as an afterthought.

"Yes, I heard that your folks moved to Scottsdale when your father retired." I was hoping to steer the conversation to other matters. "How do they like it there?"

"It's fine. They were tired of the snow and cold. Scottsdale is so much more..." She stopped, searching for the right word.

"Snooty?" I asked, cocking my head to one side. Pine Mountain is more cowboy boots and jeans than high heels and pearls. Her mother had lamented the lack of cultural activities here ten years ago.

"No, I wouldn't put it quite like that." She was horrified at my suggestion. "People with more..." She stopped again. She was digging a deeper hole for herself with each word. Finally she gave up looking.

"Refinement," I offered another suggestion. This time she nodded her head. "I was surprised that you didn't move with them. In school, you said you couldn't wait to leave this "small town" in the dust." I put finger quotes around the words she always said with a sneer.

"Well, things change." Before I could say anything else, she rushed on with the reason for her visit. "I was surprised to hear that Jim had his usual Thanksgiving Day party. Since Hannah was born, Jane hasn't felt like hosting any parties. How was it?"

"It wasn't a party. There were just a few friends and family. Jim is still in mourning since Max was killed."

"Oh, yes, I understand. It is so horrible." Her tone didn't match her expression. "He must be devastated about his brother's activities. Who wouldn't be? Everyone at the bank is still in mourning at the passing of young Fred as well. We can't imagine why anyone would kill such a nice man." I made a point of looking at the clock on the wall. I didn't want her sitting here all day even though we weren't busy.

She abruptly changed topics again. "We never did get a chance to go out for lunch. Are you free today? The library closes at noon, right?" Was this the real reason for her visit? What exactly was she hoping to discover? Unless I told another lie, I was stuck.

The phone on my desk rang before I could come up with an excuse. "Excuse me, Beth Ann." Saved by the bell, I thought as I picked up the phone. I turned slightly away from her for a little privacy. "Pine Mountain Library, This is Miss Foster. How may I help you?"

"Would you like to join me for lunch today, Holly?" Linda whispered. Surprised, I looked up. She was standing at the front desk with her back to me. She had heard Beth Ann asking about lunch and came to my rescue. "I hope I'm not overstepping my bounds."

"Not at all, that sounds great." I tried to keep the relief out of my voice. "I'll have the research ready for you first thing Monday." It was the only thing I could think of to say. That wasn't exactly a lie either. I did plan on doing some research over the weekend, but it wasn't for a student.

Replacing the phone, I turned back to Beth Ann with a smile. "Sorry for the interruption. Now where were we?"

"We were making arrangements to meet for lunch today." She seemed impatient now.

"I'm sorry, but I already have plans. We'll have to do it another time. I really need to get to work on that research now." I stood up, hoping she'd take the hint.

"Yes, of course," she sighed. "Are you free tomorrow? The library isn't open on Sunday." She wasn't going to let this go.

"Tomorrow is Hannah's first birthday. Jim is having a small birthday party for her at the ranch after church. Just for the family," I added in case she thought I would invite her. I was grateful I didn't have to lie about that.

"Maybe another time," Beth Ann huffed. She was miffed now. She didn't like having her plans thwarted. Looking for gossip was one thing, but I didn't understand her sudden interest in being my friend.

Waiting until Beth Ann's car left the parking lot, Linda came over to my desk. "I don't recall her ever coming in here before, not even when she was a student. I hope you don't mind that I did that."

"Certainly not. You saved me from telling a lie to get out of lunch with her. Is the diner fine with you?"

"Oh, we don't really have to have lunch together. Unless you want to, that is." She was embarrassed now. I didn't know much about her personal life. She never talked about any family in town.

"I think it's a great idea. Besides, she's the type to be watching to see if I really do have plans," I said. "I'd rather not get caught in a lie." A smile lit up her face as she went back to her desk. I felt bad that I hadn't made an effort to get to know her until now. On several occasions I'd gotten the impression she was alone and lonely.

Christmas shopping had slacked off from the previous day, and several people came in to check out books. The library also had good internet service, and people came in to use the computers for online shopping. I had updated the security system when I first started working at the library. I didn't want anyone using the library's computers to have their identity stolen or their accounts hacked.

I wondered if the bank had discovered how poor their security was. They really needed to do something about it. If the money had been taken because of their lack of security, I wasn't sure how that could be proven.

I didn't know if Fred had been part of the theft, but why else had he been killed? My questions, no matter how innocent I thought they had been, must have made someone nervous. They had decided he was expendable. That would always be on my head.

Max said to follow the clues. But I hadn't found any clues to follow. I'd run out of ideas where he could have left what he wanted me to find. I didn't even know what a clue would look like. After the break-in at my house, I had gone through every closet, cupboard, and drawer. Everything in them belonged to me.

Staring at my blank computer screen, I sighed. I wanted to help clear Max's name, but I didn't know how. Hacking into the bank's records was out of the question. Drake would arrest me for sure if I was caught.

I'd checked out the town's web site several times. The only interesting piece of information I found was the name of the man Jane had spent so much time with on Thanksgiving. Wendell Kramer worked in the town's IT department. That meant he knew his way around computers. Had he known about the poor security at the bank, and used it to his advantage?

Max said it had started out as a game, but he didn't say what the game was, or who was playing. I felt like I was going in circles.

Drake said Jack Johnston, the Assistant Treasurer, had alerted Jim about the missing money. Why had he been checking the accounts even before anyone knew Max was missing? What had he been looking for? Had something made him suspicious? Or was he trying to point the finger away from himself?

Looking at the town's web site again, I studied the picture of Jack Johnston. He looked to be in his fifties with thinning brown hair. His online bio gave very little information other than his work history. He'd worked for the town in one department or another most of his adult life.

What if he'd been hoping to get the treasurer's job when Jim gave it to Max? He could have framed Max in order to open up the position again. It might be a good idea to check further into Jack Johnston.

Concentrating on the screen, I wasn't aware someone had stepped up to my desk. Nearly jumping out of my chair, I whirled around to find Drake staring down at me. "Checking something out?" He didn't look happy at what was on my computer screen.

My face felt like it was on fire, but I tried to bluff my way through. "Yes, I was looking to see who some the guests were at your dad's dinner. I still don't know that many people in town."

"So you're looking up people who work for the town?" He cocked his head to one side.

"Well, I figured he had invited some people he worked with. Is there something wrong with that?"

"Not at all, but Dad doesn't work in the Treasurer's Office. What's really going on in that pretty head of yours, Holly?"

"Nothing sinister, I assure you." I put on my most innocent look, fluttering my eyelashes at him. "Isn't the town web site out there for people to look at? I didn't think that was a crime."

He sat down on the corner of my desk, facing me. "What are you really doing?" He kept his voice low so no one could listen in on our conversation. He picked up my hand, playing with my fingers.

"Whatever it is, it's not very helpful." I shrugged, giving up the pretense of innocently looking at the web site. "Drake, I believe Max knew who took the money. He was scared when he came to see me." I kept repeating that, hoping he would finally believe me.

"If that's the case, why didn't he tell Dad, or me? We would have helped him in any way possible. I still don't understand why he came to you."

"Does it bruise your ego that he came to me instead of you?" I tugged my hand free of his grasp, as my temper began to heat up.

"My ego is a little sturdier than that." He chuckled. "Why don't you tell me what you're really up to?"

I released a sigh. "Max wasn't behind that big store deal either, but someone who worked for the town was. I just want to figure out who would benefit from doing that."

He leaned over, whispering in my ear. "Give it a rest. I've got this covered."

I jerked back, surprise written on my face. Before I could say anything, he placed his finger over my lips. "Don't say anything. There are ears everywhere." He looked across the lobby where a group of women were sitting. They came in every week to discuss the latest book they were reading. They weren't interested in their books right now. They were intently watching us.

"You know who did it?" My voice was barely above a whisper.

"I know my job, and I know how to investigate. I need you to stay out of things. I don't want you to get hurt. Is that so hard to understand?" I shook my head. "Good. I'm doing everything to find the money, and put things right."

"I know, but I don't understand why the bank hasn't been able to trace where the money was transferred to. They should have found out what happened almost immediately. What's the hold up?"

"It's not that simple. Someone rerouted the money before it even left the bank here. It never made it to the embezzler's account." He ran his fingers through his hair in frustration.

"Max," I whispered. "He did that. He said to follow the trail."

"Trail?" Drake sat back, looking at me. "I thought he said to follow the clues."

"Well, yeah, or the trail. What difference does it make?"

"That's two different things." He leaned down, kissing me soundly. "Thanks. I'll take it from here." He tapped the end of my nose with one finger. "Stay out of trouble. I want you around for that formal proposal, remember?" With a final kiss, he stood up.

With a small salute and a smile to the book club women, he sauntered out of the library. Several of the ladies giggled at his antics while others waved a hand in front of their faces. The man was incorrigible. I shook my head, but couldn't help but smile. My heart was tripping happily in my chest.

Linda came over to my desk a few minutes later. "Is

everything all right? I'll understand if you need to cancel our lunch."

"Everything's fine and we're not canceling lunch."

Looking at the door where he disappeared, she smiled softly. "He's a good man, much like his father. Both of his boys are good men." I couldn't agree more, but I didn't say anything.

We had fifteen minutes before closing for the weekend. First Beth Ann, and now Drake, I was ready for this day to be over.

The diner was busy when Linda and I walked in a half hour later. People were tired of eating leftover turkey, but didn't want to go to the trouble of cooking. Dennis and Darlene's three grandkids were sitting at the counter, the youngest in a high chair. Cheerios were scattered on the high chair tray, and the other two were eating French fries. Their daughter Debbie was waiting tables while their son-in-law Mike was in the kitchen with Dennis filling orders.

Their diner was one of the businesses that would suffer if chain stores and restaurants began taking over the town. There was a lot to be said for family businesses that chains couldn't offer.

When a table opened up at the back of the busy diner, Linda and I took our seats. An awkward silence settled over us. We'd never socialized before, and I wasn't sure how to begin. Drawing a deep breath, I asked the question that had been plaguing me recently. "Did you apply for the position Jim gave me?" If that had been the case, it might account for her stilted attitude towards me at times.

"No," she frowned. "Why do you ask?"

"You've worked at the library for a long time. It stands to reason that you might have wanted the promotion."

She gave me a shy smile. "Yes, I've been there a long time, long enough to know that I don't want to be the boss. I can go home at night and not worry about all the administrative duties you have to deal with. The student books alone are a nightmare.

"Then there's the students themselves." She shook her head. "Most of them are very nice and well-behaved. That isn't the case with all of them though. The parents are even worse." She shuddered slightly. "You don't have to worry. I'm not after your job. That headache is all yours."

"Thanks, I think." I laughed. I knew exactly what she was talking about. I'd already had a run-in with a couple of parents who thought their son or daughter could do no wrong.

"As long as I enjoy what I'm doing, I'm content," she continued quietly. "When my husband died, he left me with a nice nest egg, and my house is paid for. I don't have to worry about finances." Her dark eyes clouded over with a deep sadness. "Money doesn't keep me warm on cold nights, but it pays the electric bill."

She gave a small gasp, and her mouth dropped open. I started to turn around, but she stopped me. "Beth Ann just walked in. I guess you were right. She's checking to make sure you really did have plans."

You could hear a pin drop as she walked across the small room. Ignoring the other customers, she marched over to our table. "Well, hello." She gave us a frosty smile. "Is this a business meeting?"

"Of course not. Why would you think that?" My smile felt stiff on my face.

"I don't think I've ever seen the two of you socializing before. Maybe this was a spur of the moment thing?" She looked between us. Linda seemed paralyzed in her seat. Her eyes were as big as dollars. Getting caught in a lie wasn't a good position to be in.

"What are you suggesting, Beth Ann?" I asked, deciding the best offense is defense. I wasn't going to let her make me feel guilty. "Linda and I work together. Is there any reason we can't be friends as well? Most people become friends with the people they work with."

"Well, I thought you were probably lying about being busy

to avoid going to lunch with me." Her tone was aggressive. She didn't bother to keep her voice down.

I didn't know what to say to that, and an awkward silence settled over us. I could feel the stares of the other customers. They seemed to be holding their collective breaths. "Are you ladies ready to order?" Darlene casually approached our table. She propped her hand on her hip, a playful smile tugging at her lips.

"Um sure," Linda finally found her tongue. "Would you like to join us, Beth Ann?" Her gracious question shocked Beth Ann as much as it did Darlene and me.

"Oh! Um, sure." She pulled out the spare chair.

"All right then." Darlene was the first to recover from this turn of events. "Our special today is grilled ham and cheese on rye with French fries or onion rings. I don't have gluten-free bread." She gave Beth Ann an apologetic smile. "Do you have allergies like your mother? She was allergic to almost everything we serve, and was never able to eat here."

Beth Ann ignored the snarkiness in her tone. "No, I don't have any allergies, but thank you for asking. The special sounds great. I'll have the fries." Linda and I agreed on the special as well, and Darlene bustled off.

We were all silent waiting for someone to speak. Customers at the other tables were quiet as well. No one wanted to say something that would be embellished and repeated. This was torture, and I couldn't wait for it to end.

But Linda and I weren't the only ones eager for the meal to be over. Beth Ann finished her sandwich in record time, and pushed back her chair. "Thanks for inviting me to join you. It's been…fun. Maybe we can do it again sometime." She hurried out the door before we could say anything. Everyone in the diner seemed to give a sigh of relief once she was out the door.

It wasn't until she was gone that Linda and I realized she'd left us with the tab for her meal. I had to laugh. "Well, that was certainly an interesting meal, but I wouldn't call it fun."

Linda nodded agreement. "I'm sorry I asked her to join us, but I couldn't think of a way to get around it. Since it was my idea, I'll pay for her meal."

"Nonsense, we can split it." I laughed. "To think I was starting to feel sorry for her."

Darlene walked up to the table with the tickets in her hand, looking at Beth Ann's empty chair. "That was about the most awkward meal I've ever witnessed in my diner. I don't know what surprises me more, the fact that you asked her to join you, or that she stuck you with paying for her meal." She shook her head. "Actually, that part doesn't surprise me. I really thought she'd leave when I came to take your orders. That's the first time she's eaten in our lowly establishment."

"I really didn't think she'd agree to join us, or I wouldn't have suggested it." Linda gave a little shudder. "She is just like her mother, and that woman scared me to death."

Darlene let out a loud laugh. "Don't let her know that. You'll be in her sights for the rest of your life." She tore up all three lunch tickets. "This one's on me. It was worth it to see her tongue-tied for a change. Would you like some dessert? Maybe you can actually enjoy part of the meal." She gave another boisterous laugh.

CHAPTER FOURTEEN

"It's gone," He had to work hard to keep from yelling.
"What's gone?"
"What the hell do you think? Our money, it's gone."
"How can that be? Where did it go?"
"If I knew that, I could just get it back." He started pacing, trying to work off some of the agitation bottled up inside him. How had he gotten himself into this mess?
"No one but Max and Fred knew what you were doing, so how could it be gone? Where would it go?"
"No, they weren't the only ones to know what we were doing," he said. "You knew." He didn't want to tell her about Max's lover. That would create a whole new problem.
"Are you seriously accusing me of taking the money? How could you even think that? It was supposed to be for us to start our life together." There were tears in her voice now.
"I'm sorry, honey. You know I didn't mean it like that." He was silent for several minutes trying to make sense of this. Where could the money have gone?
"Are you sure it got transferred? You did check it, right?"
"I took Fred's word that the transfer went through."
"What? Why didn't you check it when you knew Max was on to you?"
"What could he do once the transfer was made? It was a numbered account with passcodes and everything."
"Yet the money is missing. What are we going to do now?"
"It has to be that damned librarian. Max said he left evidence, and he'd been to see her. She's the only one who could have taken it."
"Then we'll have to do something to get it back. I'm tired of this town. I want out of here." Before he could think of an answer, she disconnected the call.

~~~

Drake showed up on my doorstep with a pizza, a bottle of wine, and a six-pack of beer. The last time he brought wine it was a peace offering. What was the excuse now? Did he have more bad news? Coming in, he placed a kiss on my lips before going to the kitchen with his offerings.

"What's the occasion?" I asked as he set the bottle down on my kitchen table. One glass of wine was my limit. If he drank the entire six-pack, he wouldn't be fit to drive home. He'd spent one night on my couch before he installed the new locks. I thought that was enough to teach him not to try it again. Until I could buy a new couch, I was stuck with the one I had while in college. It had seen better days.

"No occasion, just a simple dinner. The wine is for you, the beer is for me, the pizza is for both of us. I hope you still like pepperoni pizza with extra cheese." I was in love with him, but there was still a lot we needed to know about each other before we could move forward. Hopefully that wouldn't take long.

"What's this I hear about you having lunch with Beth Ann today?" He chuckled at the thought. "What did she want?"

"I'm not really sure. It was the most uncomfortable half hour I've spent in forever." I shook my head. "No one said more than a few words once she came into the diner."

"Don't let her fool you," he warned. "She'll pump you for information then use it against you. Did she ask a lot of questions about the case?"

"Like I said, we barely talked. I thought I was going to have indigestion from eating so fast. We just wanted it to end. I was with Linda when Beth Ann came into the diner. She was checking up on me."

He looked up from opening the bottle of wine. "Checking up on you? What's that about?"

I explained about Beth Ann's visit to the library that morning. "Linda heard her ask me to go to lunch with her, and called my desk to ask me to lunch before I gave my answer to Beth Ann. She thought I was lying, so I guess she followed me to the diner."

He frowned at me. "That's bordering on stalking. Why would she do that?"

I shrugged. I didn't want to talk about Beth Ann any longer. "Did you really figure out who started this whole thing with Dynamic Corporation? Or was that just a way to keep me from snooping?"

"I've got it taken care of. In fact, Mr. Fletcher came to my office to let me know they weren't going to pursue building a store in town."

That sounded a little ominous to me. "So where are they going to try to build it?" I picked up my glass, taking a sip of the sweet white wine. He didn't answer my question.

"I don't really care as long as it isn't in Pine Mountain." Without waiting for a plate, he took a big bite out of his slice of pizza.

"You might want to check with the County Supervisors. Since he didn't get what he wanted in town, he might try something outside of town. That would have the same effect on the local stores."

"Damn, I hadn't thought of that." He put down his pizza, pulling his phone off his belt. "I might have to hire you as one of my detectives." He gave me a wink.

"Who are you calling? You won't be able to get any of the supervisors on a Saturday night."

"Hi, Dad, you might want to check with the County Supervisors first thing Monday morning." He explained about my theory. Talking this over for several minutes, he asked another question before he hung up. "How are things there?" He listened, shaking his head. "Yeah, okay. I'll see you in the morning."

"What was that about?"

"Things don't look good right now out at the ranch. Jane won't tell him where she spent Thanksgiving night and has locked him out of their bedroom. If she tries to take Hannah away, he'll fight her with everything he has. This is the first time he's admitted how bad things are."

"I can guess where she was and who she was with."

"How?" His eyebrows lowered over his eyes.

"When I was looking at the town's web site I saw the man she spent so much time with on Thanksgiving Day. If Jane didn't spend the night at the ranch, I'd say she went somewhere with that guy. How could she do that to Jim?"

"Never mind about Dad, he's a big boy. He got himself into this mess. How could she take off with some guy and leave Hannah all night?" Anger tinged his voice. "What's the guy's name? You said you saw him on the town website?" I nodded my head. "What department?" He shot the questions at me as he paced.

"His name is Wendell something. He was with Jane every time I saw her after the argument in the kitchen. Why would Jim invite him?"

"I doubt that he did. There were only a couple of people from the mayor's office at the ranch. The others were from the store. If she was spending that much time with the guy, she probably invited him. Do you know what department he works for?"

"The IT department. That would give him access to all sorts of things. He might even be able to pick up passcodes to the bank. That's what Max wanted me to find."

"Damn," he swore again. "Can you find his last name for me? If he's behind the embezzlement, he's also a killer."

My heart was pounding in my ears. "Do you think Jane knew what he was doing?"

He shook his head. "I'm not going to jump to any conclusions yet. That's where everyone went wrong in the first place. We all assumed Max was at fault." I cleared my throat, and he gave me a small smile. "Okay, you and Bill were the only ones willing to give him the benefit of a doubt. I should have known better. That is one thing we're taught at the academy, follow the evidence and don't assume anything." He shook his head in frustration. "Find that guy's last name for me. I'll start there."

I opened up my laptop. I hadn't used it since the night of Jim's first town hall meeting. Whenever I needed to look something up, I used the computer at the library or my tablet. "What's going on?" I muttered, staring at the screen. The icons on the desktop had been rearranged.

"What's the matter?" Drake looked over my shoulder.

"Everything is moved around. Someone has used my laptop."

"Maybe there was an automatic update that changed things. Don't worry about it now. Check out that guy's last name for me."

Studying the different icons, I shook my head. Updates wouldn't rearrange things on the screen. Someone broke into my house. A burglar would steal my laptop, not mess with it. I looked at Drake. "There's a new folder on the desktop." I frowned at the screen trying to decide what to do. "Max told me to follow the trail. I don't know how long he'd been in my house before I got home. I don't take my laptop to work with me every day because I have access to anything I need at the library."

Moving the curser over the new file, my heart beat faster. "This is it," I whispered. "It has to be." I started to click on it, when Drake put his hand on mine.

"What if it wasn't Max who put it there? Whoever killed him beat him first. What if the killer made him tell where he put his evidence? There could be a virus on that file that will destroy your computer. You'd lose anything Max sent you along with anything you have on there. Can you isolate that folder from the rest of your computer?"

I shook my head. "I would need an external hard drive for that. I'm not equipped to do that here."

"Okay, for now leave that file alone. Look up Wendell's last name so I can check him out."

I pulled up the town's website to find Wendell's last name. Then remotely logging on to the Police Department's computer, Drake plugged Wendell Kramer's name into system. Fifteen minutes later, he leaned back with a frustrated sigh. "The guy looks squeaky clean. He doesn't even have a parking ticket to his name."

"That doesn't mean he didn't do this," I argued. "It just means he hasn't been caught at something. Besides, he isn't exactly squeaky clean. Whatever else he's done, he's having an affair with Jane," I said with disgust.

"We don't know that's what's going on with them. I don't like her any more than you do, but I'm trying to keep an open mind. I've learned my lesson. I'm not going to assume anyone is guilty until I have all the evidence."

I understood where he was coming from. Jane isn't a very good mother, but that doesn't mean she is involved with embezzlement and murder. He hadn't convinced me that she wasn't having an affair though. "Whatever happens with Jane, I feel sorry for Hannah. She deserves a better mother than the one she has. Is your dad still going to have the birthday party tomorrow? Will Jane even bother to be there?"

He shrugged. "Your guess is as good as mine. We've done all we can do tonight. Can we discuss something that won't ruin our dinner?" He had already eaten two big pieces of pizza. What was left was cold. I turned on the oven to warm it up. Some people don't mind cold pizza, but I'm not one of them.

Picking up the beer he'd set aside, he drained it in one gulp. It looked like he might be spending the night on my couch again. It wouldn't be good if the Chief of Police was picked up for DUI on his way home.

He finished off the last of the pizza, and we went into the living room. While he watched football, I opened my Kindle hoping to forget all the problems plaguing our town. It didn't work. My mind kept churning, trying to sort things out. I finally gave up, setting it aside.

I wished I had an external hard drive at home, but that would have to wait until I got to work on Monday. There were several spare drives I could use to transfer the folder from my laptop. I didn't want to take any chances of releasing a virus that would destroy my computer.

Drake said he knew who sent the original emails to Dynamic Corporation. I stopped that thought. No, he said he had it under control. I wasn't sure what that meant.

"Did the same person that embezzled the money contact Dynamic about building a store here? Or was it two different people?" He was lost in the game. I had to wait until half time for my chance to ask my questions.

"All I have right now is circumstantial," he said with a sigh. "Fletcher said Dynamic thought they were dealing with the town treasurer. I'll call Dynamic first thing Monday morning to see if there is anything else they can tell me. Dad informed the County Supervisors about a possible bid to build there. Most of the land outside of town is either National Forest, private property, or county and state land. There isn't anything we can do about a private owner selling their land to whoever they want. National Forest and state land is a different matter."

"Who would benefit most from one of those stores being built around here?" I asked. "If someone was hoping to sell their land to Dynamic, they wouldn't want the company to build in town."

"None of the current store owners would welcome that store in town or just outside. Their businesses would all end up closing. I've seen it happen in other small towns. I don't want that to happen here."

"Max kept telling me to follow the trail. Were you able to figure out what he meant?"

"I can't follow something if I don't know where I'm supposed to look. I hope that folder you found is what we're looking for." He raked his fingers through his hair causing it to fall over his forehead. I reached up, following the path his fingers had made. I loved the silky texture of the thick strands. Drake missed most of the second half of the football game.

~~~

Sunday morning was cold, but sunny. June and Jill hijacked me before I got to the steps of the church. "Have you checked out Facebook this morning?" The question came out of left field.

"No, I don't check Facebook on a daily basis. Why? Did someone post something about me?" Social media wasn't my favorite form of communication.

"Well, not directly," June hedged cryptically.

"Okay, it's too cold to stand out here and play games. What are you two talking about?" I had started to shiver.

"Beth Ann posted that she had a very informative lunch with someone close to the police chief. That could only be you." Jill gave me a sly wink. "Why didn't you tell us you had lunch with her yesterday? Why would you even do that? What were you thinking?"

I groaned. "Believe me, it wasn't my idea. Did she say what was so informative about this lunch?" My temper heated me from the inside out, and I no longer felt the cold wind. "Why would she post that she had lunch with someone? No one cares who she ate with."

"Well, she cares," June stated. "She said there would be wedding bells soon. Is there any truth to that?"

"Nothing has been said about a wedding." Technically, that was the truth. Drake still had to make his 'formal proposal.' They seemed disappointed at that. "Nothing was said about Drake. In fact, very little was said. We ate, and she left. She didn't even pay for her own lunch. It was the most awkward meal I've ever sat through. What else did she post?" I held my breath.

The twins shared a look before saying anything more. "She hinted that her lunch buddy was helping the police find a killer and the town's missing money." June said, giving her head a shake. The wind blew her long hair into her face. "I can't believe how much money the thief got away with. I didn't know the town had that much money."

"She even posted how much was taken?" The twins

nodded their heads in unison. "How could she do that? Any information about accounts at the bank is confidential. If she isn't careful she'll lose her job." That was the least of my worries.

"I guess she doesn't care about that," Jill shrugged. "She promised to keep everyone apprised of what's happening in the romance department as well as the investigation."

I hung my head. I didn't know whether I should cry or scream. "Absolutely nothing was said about any romance. I didn't tell her anything about Drake's investigation because I don't know anything. Drake would never share information about one of his cases with me or anyone else. She made it all up. He's going to kill me." I shook my head. "I mean that figuratively," I added quickly.

"To think Linda and I felt sorry for her," I muttered softly. The wind had picked up since I stepped out of my car, blowing my short strawberry blonde hair into my face. I shook it away, looking off towards the front of the church where Drake was waiting for me.

"Linda was with you and Beth Ann?" they chorused. "She didn't say anything about there being three of you at lunch," Jill added.

"Lucky Linda," I said. "We went to the diner after the library closed. It was supposed to be a nice, casual lunch. Beth Ann interrupted us before we could even give our order. We couldn't very well let her stand there and watch us eat." I hated to think what Beth Ann would have to say if she realized Linda was secretly in love with Jim. She would have a field day with that piece of news.

I was beginning to shiver again from the cold as much as with anger. How could she post a bunch of lies like that? "I'm going inside and ask God to forgive me for the hateful thoughts I'm having right now." I stomped off, leaving the twins behind.

"What was that all about?" Drake nodded towards the parking lot as he dropped a soft kiss on my lips.

"I don't want to talk about it right now. I'm going to church." I moved past him, my back held rigid with anger. It wouldn't surprise me if smoke was coming out of my ears, I was that mad.

~~~

"*She knows. She found whatever Max had on us. She has to be the one who took our money*" He had the phone propped between his shoulder and ear as he paced. "*We have to stop her before she turns us in.*"

"*Calm down,*" she urged. "*If she knew anything, she would have already told Drake. We just need to remain calm.*"

"*No!*" He was almost shouting now. "*I'm not going to jail. We need to leave now.*"

"*We can't leave without the money,*" she stated matter-of-factly. "*Everyone assumed Max was guilty because he disappeared. It won't be any different if we disappear. People will think we're guilty as well.*"

"*We are guilty.*" *His voice raised several decibels.*

"*You need to find where she put the money, and get it back. You can still turn this around. We need that money, or we'll be stuck here forever.*"

CHAPTER FIFTEEN

"You were mad enough to spit nails when you walked up the steps. What had you going?" Drake walked me to my car after the service. After dropping my car off at my place, we were going to the ranch for Hannah's birthday party.

"You're not going to like it." I drew a deep breath. "Maybe we should wait until we get to my place. I have to check something out on my laptop."

"Why so mysterious?" He frowned.

"Because June and Jill told me Beth Ann posted something on Facebook that I want to check out."

"Such as?" The muscle in his jaw twitched as he gritted his teeth. Beth Ann had that effect on people.

"That woman is a menace," he grumbled, but he didn't push me for an immediate answer. "I'll follow you to your place." He stomped over to his truck.

I couldn't get on Beth Ann's Facebook page since I'd never 'friended' her. There were plenty of people who had shared her latest post though. Drake sat beside me on the couch as we scrolled down the page. "Talk about fake news," I said. "The only thing she put in here that isn't a lie is that she was at DD's Diner for lunch yesterday. She didn't have to give my name since everyone in town knows about us. She left out the part about Linda being there. Does she think she can get away with posting so many lies?"

"As long as she didn't name names, no one can complain or contradict her. That's how those gossip rags at the grocery store get away with what they print."

"I hope you know I would never repeat anything you told me about the investigation." I looked at him beseechingly. "Everything she said was a lie."

He pulled me close for a hug. "I'm not worried about that, but I am worried that the killer will read this, and take it for gospel. If he thinks you know who he is, he's going to come after you."

My stomach twisted with that thought. "If he believes this pack of lies, won't he leave town before you can arrest him? Wouldn't he think I'd already given you any evidence I found?"

"That's being overly optimistic. We can't take the chance that whoever the guilty party is will take off. It would be an admission of guilt if someone close to the case suddenly left town." He paced around my living room. "Beth Ann doesn't realize how much danger she's put you in, or the trouble she's in. The bank isn't going to be happy with her for releasing information about the embezzlement, even though she exaggerated the amount that went missing."

As much as I wanted to post a snarky reply, I decided that would only give credence to her words. If she was hoping to get a rise out of me, she was going to be disappointed. As hard as it was to do, ignoring her would be better.

When the clock on the mantle chimed the hour, I closed down my laptop. "We need to get out to the ranch, or we'll be late for the party." I hesitated, looking around the room. "Where can I hide this?" I held up the laptop.

"Good idea." Although he had replaced all the locks with dead bolts, neither of us wanted to take a chance with any potential evidence that might be on my computer. "Take it with us," he said. "We can put it in the storage space under the cargo area in my SUV."

With the laptop safely concealed, we headed for the ranch. "Where was Jane this morning?" Once again, she hadn't come with Jim and Hannah.

"Dad said she was busy getting ready for the party. I'm not sure how many people she was planning on attending this gala. You'd think this was Hannah's coming out party instead of her first birthday."

During the short drive, my thoughts returned to Beth Ann's post. What would the killer do if he read it? Would he really come after me? My stomach filled with nervous butterflies.

The house was already getting crowded when we arrived at the ranch. Jane was acting the gracious hostess, passing out air kisses to everyone, even me. This was a quickly planned event since Jim had originally meant to hold the party on Thanksgiving Day. I wondered how Jane had managed to pull this together.

I gave Drake a curious look after she planted a real kiss on the corner of his lips. "Is she drunk or high?" I whispered after she moved on. I'd never seen her quite this outgoing.

He shrugged, and walked over to the bar. There were five bottles of wine sitting out, but no coffee and no beer. This was more up-scale than beer and pretzels. Were we supposed to start drinking before noon? When Jim came in from the kitchen, he stopped to look around, giving his head a shake. "Where's the birthday girl?" I asked softly when he joined Drake and me beside the bar.

"I put her down for a nap when I brought her home from church. She should still be sleeping, but she isn't in her crib now." Worry clouded his eyes as he scanned the crowd. "I don't see her anywhere." Jane was still making the rounds through the guests. She already had a glass of wine in her hand.

Bill joined us a few minutes later. After placing a kiss on my cheek he shook hands with Drake and gave his dad a hug. The jealousy he'd displayed a few days ago seemed to have disappeared. "Some party, Dad." He put the gift for Hannah on a table that was piled high with prettily wrapped boxes.

"Yeah," Jim sniffed, giving his head a shake. That was his only comment.

"This is going to be the best birthday party ever," Jane cooed. Her face was flushed with excitement. "Thank you for letting me arranged this for our darling little girl." She kissed Jim on the cheek. She was seldom affectionate towards him unless she wanted something. "She'll never forget this," she gushed. I wanted to remind her that Hannah was only one. She wouldn't remember it at all.

"Speaking of our little girl, where is she?" Jim asked. "I put her down for a nap, but she isn't in her crib, and I don't see her out here." He frowned at her.

"She was too excited to sleep. I think my mom has her."

"Your mom is here?" This surprised him. He looked around the room again.

"Yes, didn't I tell you she was coming? She didn't want to miss her granddaughter's first birthday. She drove in from Denver with some of my friends while you were at church. Oh, here are more guests. You'll have to excuse me." She rushed away to greet the new arrivals.

"Who are all these people?"

Giving a sigh, he shrugged his broad shoulders. "I have no idea. I don't know any of her friends from Denver. I can't believe they came all that way for a toddler's birthday party. I don't know what she was thinking." He shook his head. "Or if she even was. This was supposed to be a small party for the family, not a huge undertaking." I didn't know what Jane's game was, but she wasn't making points with her husband.

In a small rural town, people are more down to earth than in large cities. Still, everyone who was someone in Pine Mountain had been invited. Jane was out to impress people.

My mouth dropped open when Wendell Kramer came in. If he was having an affair with Jane, it took a lot of nerve to show his face here. He stopped to look around. Seeing someone across the room, a smile lit up his face. I followed his gaze, but there were too many people to know who he was looking at. With a determined step, he disappeared in the crowd.

Caterers brought in trays of finger food, and wine flowed like water. This bash had to be costing Jim a small fortune. When it was finally time to cut the birthday cake, an older woman came in with the birthday girl. I didn't know where she had been keeping her, but Hannah didn't look happy. Her big blue eyes swam with tears. Seeing her daddy, she held out her arms, her bottom lip jutted out in a pout.

Handing the baby over to Jim, the woman joined us at the edge of the crowd. "I'm so happy Jane made it possible for me to make it here for this. I haven't been able to spend as much time as I'd like with my granddaughter."

I looked up at Drake. He shrugged, but didn't say what both of us were thinking. Supposedly Jane had spent three weeks in Denver with her mother a short time ago. It appeared June was right; Jane had been in Phoenix instead. This was further proof that she was having an affair.

The crowd stood around while Jim coaxed Hannah to blow out the single candle on the big cake. She began to cry when he tried to place her in the high chair. She stiffened her back refusing to bend so he could sit her down.

"Can't you make her sit down?" Jane hissed when she came up behind him. "People are staring at us. How is it going to look if she has a temper tantrum in front of everyone?"

"About the way it looked when you had a temper tantrum on Thanksgiving Day," he snapped, not bothering to keep his voice down.

"Just get her in that chair so the caterer can cut the cake." She looked around, aware of the number of people listening to them.

"She's tired. I'll hold her. She should have had a nap when I brought her home." He turned his back on his wife.

A young man working for the caterer cut the cake, giving the first piece to Jim for Hannah. The sight of the pretty frosting flower captured her attention. She reached out for it, grabbing it with her pudgy fingers.

Caught by surprise when it smashed in her hand, her bottom lip quivered. When Jim scooped a bit of frosting off her fingers and put it in her mouth, she gave a watery smile. That was all the incentive she needed. She began licking her fingers, babbling happily.

"She's going to get her pretty dress stained with food coloring." Jane attempted to wipe Hannah's fingers, making her cry again.

"This is her party. Leave her alone. She's having fun." Jane huffed, but didn't argue.

Opening the gifts was another ordeal. She didn't care about the gifts, but the wrapping paper and boxes were a lot of fun.

A child's birthday party wasn't much fun for a bunch of adults. I didn't know how many had come from Denver. They either had a long drive ahead of them, or they had to get to the airport in Flagstaff for their return flight. By the time the last gift was opened, everyone was ready to leave. Jane's mother tried to take Hannah from Jim, drawing a squall from the baby. She wanted no part of that.

"I'm putting her down for a nap," Jim announced loudly. Turning to the guests, he gave a tight smile. "Thank you all for coming. I appreciate you spending part of your weekend with us to celebrate Hannah's first birthday. Thank you." Jane's face was bright red. She was almost foaming at the mouth with anger.

"I don't know about you guys, but I've had all the fun I can stand for one day." Bill chuckled. "I'm going to say goodbye to Dad." We followed along. We were ready to leave as well.

"Did you see Wendell Kramer? I can't believe the nerve it took to come here." We were alone in his truck, and finally able to relax. The tension had been thick enough to cut with a knife.

"Yeah, I saw him." He released a heavy sigh. "We don't know what's going on between them," Drake reminded me. "Maybe they're just friends."

I didn't argue the point, but I didn't believe it either. "I'll give you that. But Jane told your dad she was in Denver with her mom. We know better now. June said she saw her in Phoenix when she was supposed to be in Denver."

He raised his eyebrow at me. "Really? When did she tell you this?" I couldn't believe I'd forgotten about that. There was too much going on to remember everything.

He wasn't happy that I hadn't told him this earlier, but it really didn't have anything to do with the murders or the missing money. I decided to try a question of my own. "Have you asked Jack Johnston about the emails to Dynamic Corporation?"

He didn't answer right away, and I waited silently, putting the pressure on him to either answer, or tell me to butt out. He finally nodded his head, and answered my question. "I asked him about those emails. He said the first he knew about that deal was when Dad announced it at the meeting."

"Do you believe him? What about the signatures on the letters? I would bet money that Max didn't sign them. If Jack Johnston wanted the Treasurer's job, maybe he decided to get rid of a rival and punish Jim at the same time. He had all the passcodes the same as Max. He could have sent the emails to make it look like Max sent them, and transferred the money out of the town's accounts."

He gave a small chuckle. "That's a pretty good conspiracy theory you have going there."

Ignoring him, I continued. "Okay, Max said it started out as a game, but he didn't say who he was playing with or what kind of game. When things took a wrong turn and the money went missing for real, he knew who was playing. Maybe that's what's on my laptop." I paused, thinking this through. "Have any other town employees left recently? Who would benefit by that store being built in town? It would ruin so many families."

"I'm sorry, Holly. I don't have a lot of answers. I wish I did."

"Why hasn't the bank found the money yet?" I tilted my head to look up at him. "Someone has to know something." I fell silent for a moment. "What if Beth Ann is behind the money transfers? She posted about the missing money. It could be a smoke screen to keep people from looking at her."

"So why was Fred killed if Beth Ann was responsible?" He was playing devil's advocate.

I had to think about that for a minute. "Maybe they were in it together. She made a point of telling him that I was Jim's step-daughter when she introduced me. That made him very nervous."

"I think you've been reading too many mysteries." He chuckled. "Most crimes aren't that complicated."

"Then why does it take so long to solve them? They can't all be straight forward and simple."

"True, but you're looking at this as though it's a giant conspiracy. I'll give you another theory. What if Max was involved in both the embezzling and the deal with the store? Someone discovered what he was doing, and threatened to go to Jim. That's when Max cooked up this story about some game he was playing."

I was shaking my head before he finished. "Why is he dead and not the person who figured out what he was doing? Why is Fred dead?" I turned in the seat so I was facing him. "Max was scared when he came to my house. I don't believe he did any of this."

"I know you don't, and neither do I. But he was also very good at convincing people he didn't do anything wrong. Holly, I've known him all of my life. He was a manipulator. He would say and do anything to get out of a jam."

"You saw the differences in those signatures. I thought you believed Max was innocent." My temper was beginning to boil over.

"Holly, I do believe he was innocent." He reached out to take my hand. "I'm just trying to point out a few discrepancies in your conspiracy."

"If Fred was involved, why hasn't the bank done something about getting the money back?"

Pulling into my driveway and shutting off the engine, he turned to face me. "An auditor has been going over the town's accounts. This didn't just start. Someone had been manipulating the accounts over several months, if not a couple of years. It was always small amounts and made to look like a legitimate expense. I don't know how someone conned Max into going along. Or if he really did believe it was just a game."

He sighed heavily. "The bank is cooperating with the auditors. It looks like the money never made it to the original destination, but they can't find where it really went." He gave a frustrated sigh. "It will eventually get sorted out. Until then I need you to stay out of it."

I wasn't sure if he'd forgotten about the file on my laptop. If that was the case, I wasn't going to remind him. I'd check it out on my own. First, I had to get my laptop out of his SUV. "Max involved me whether you liked it or not." I reached for the door handle. This conversation wasn't getting us anywhere, and it was getting cold. I opened the back hatch of the SUV, lifting my laptop out.

Looking around, a creeping sensation moved up my spine. Long shadows were everywhere, and the wind whipped the trees and bushes, casting eerily moving shadows. Someone could be lurking anywhere.

Drake started towards the house, but stopped when I didn't follow him. Looking over his shoulder, he frowned. "What's wrong?" His gaze moved from me to the surrounding yard.

"Nothing I guess," I said, even as a shudder shook me.

"Get back in the truck, and give me your keys. I'll check out the house."

"No, that's not necessary. I'm being silly. Our conversation just has me spooked" I reluctantly took a step towards the house when he put his hand on my arm.

"It might not be necessary, but humor me." He held out his hand for my keys. He opened the passenger door, and helped me back inside. "Lock the doors. Keep your phone handy." He placed a soft kiss on my lips, and moved up to my back door.

I traced his movement through the house as he turned on the lights in each room. It didn't take long for him to inspect every nook and cranny. Coming back outside, he gave the all-clear. I was feeling foolish now. I'd let my imagination carry me away.

The house looked the same as it had when we left. Nothing was out of place. I flopped down on the couch, leaning my head against the back cushion. If someone had broken in, they were the neatest burglars around.

While I browsed the internet, Drake turned on the television. There were still a few football games on. Finding nothing interesting, I closed down my laptop. I wanted to know what was on the new file I'd discovered, but I didn't dare open it in case it was a virus that would wipe out my own files.

When I began to get cold, I lit a match to the kindling in the fireplace. It wouldn't take but a few minutes for the burning logs to warm up the living room. Doing nothing didn't come natural to me. It gave me too much time to think. I needed to be busy. Instead of sitting back down, I decided to do a little housecleaning.

Starting in my bedroom, I worked my way to the living room. Drake was still engrossed in the game. I didn't think he'd appreciate it if I started up the vacuum. Straightening up the papers on the coffee table, I let out a shriek when Drake grabbed me around the waist, pulling me onto his lap.

"Can't you sit still for a minute?" he whispered against my neck. He nibbled his way up to my ear, leaving a trail of goosebumps along my skin. By the time he captured my lips, I was breathless. I kept hoping we would get through learning about the adult us pretty soon, so he could get on with the formal proposal he'd mentioned.

The loud jangle of Drake's phone had us jerking apart like two teenagers caught necking on their parent's couch. "Damn," He pulled the phone off his belt. "Yeah, Cox here," he grumbled. He listened for several minutes. "All right, I'll be right there."

Running his fingers through his hair, he stood up. "I've got to go. Wally got drunk and decided he needed a few groceries."

"What's that got to do with you? Did he forget to pay for them?" I frowned up at him from my comfortable position on the couch.

"He forgot to get out of his truck before going into the store." He chuckled, but I let out a gasp. "He's lucky no one was hurt. The big window at the front of the grocery store is smashed to pieces." He shook his head. "That man will never learn. It's been a while since he pulled something like this. Every time he gets all wrapped up in the past he ties on a good drunk." The man was pathetic. I could almost feel sorry for him, but any troubles he had were all of his own doing.

Drake pulled me off the couch. "I'll call you when I can. I probably won't make it back here tonight. Will you be okay here by yourself?" He rested his forehead against mine.

"I'll be fine," I assured him. "I'll finish cleaning house so I don't have to do it during the week. Let me know what your dad finds out from the County Supervisors." If the big store was built just outside of town the result on the businesses in town would be the same. Most of them would close.

CHAPTER SIXTEEN

Driving through town the next morning, I noticed the boarded-up window at the grocery store. Wally had really done a number on it. He was lucky he hadn't spent the night in the hospital instead of the jail. I felt sorry for Bud and Arlene though. This would put a damper on their business. Maybe this would be the incentive Wally needed to get help for his problems. Or would this be one more thing he blamed Max for?

Instead of going to the library first thing Monday morning, I made a detour to the bank. When Beth Ann saw me, her face lost most of the high color leaving behind two bright red spots of blusher.

"Oh, um, hi Holly. I wasn't expecting to see you again so soon. That was some lunch we enjoyed Saturday." She was trying to bluff her way through.

"So right you are. The silence at our table was almost painful." I gave her my most menacing smile. "In fact you were in such a hurry to escape that you forgot to pay for your lunch. I'm sure Darlene would appreciate it if you stopped by to pay her today." Her face was bright red now. She looked around at the others in the lobby. Everyone was staring at us.

"Right, sure, I'll do that on my lunch break." She glared at the woman at the next desk who was obviously listening to our conversation and enjoying Beth Ann's discomfort.

"But I didn't come here to talk about our awkward lunch. I did want to know why you posted that pack of lies on Facebook." My hands were braced on my hips now. I didn't bother to keep my voice down. Confronting her in person was better than trying to refute her lies online.

"I don't know what you're talking about, Holly. Now if you'll excuse me, I need to get to work." She turned to the monitor on her desk. I wasn't to be deterred though.

"Of course you do. I just wanted you to know that Chief Cox might be stopping by to ask you a few questions."

"About what?" Her voice crackled, and the color had drained from her face again.

"About that post of course," I shrugged.

"It isn't against the law to say something on Facebook, even..." She stopped before admitting it was all a lie.

"No, I'm sure a lot of people tell lies on all of the social media sites. But he is interested in where you got your information about the amount of money that was taken out of the town's accounts. That's confidential banking information." The branch manager was standing in the doorway to his office listening to our chat. His arms were crossed over his chest, and a frown drew his thick brows together.

Beth Ann turned in his direction, panic in her eyes. "I...it was a guess. I didn't mean anything by that post. You know how social media works. Most of it is a bunch of..." She tried to think of the proper word.

"A bunch of lies, yes I know," I agreed with her. "Maybe the world would be a better place if people remembered the Golden Rule." She looked puzzled so I enlightened her. "'*Do unto others as you would have them do unto you.*'" I turned and walked out. I'd accomplished what I came for.

Linda was pacing in front of the desk when I walked in a few minutes later. I'd called her to let her know that I would be late. "What did she say? Did she admit she'd lied?" Her voice was a worried whisper. There were a few people at the tables and easy chairs. No one was paying attention to us.

"I wish you had been there." I clamped my hand over my mouth to keep from giggling out loud. "I need to call Darlene to tell her Beth Ann might be coming over to pay for the lunch she forgot about on Saturday."

Linda gave a small giggle of her own. "I would love to have seen her face on that one."

"Anyone in the bank will be checking out that post. If they haven't already seen it, that is. I think she's going to have a little trouble explaining things to her boss though." I tried to shake off the guilt that poked at me.

"Maybe she'll learn she can't make things up about people," Linda said, sounding relieved.

Checking that folder on my laptop turned out to be a confusing disappointment. It contained nothing more interesting than a bunch of screenshots of spreadsheets, accounting ledgers, and bank accounts. There were no names, only numbers to identify them. I didn't know the account numbers that belonged to the town, so I didn't know whose they were.

It was noon before I heard from Drake about Dynamic Corporation. "They weren't too happy to hear about Mr. Fletcher's visit," he chuckled. "They admitted to receiving emails from someone they thought was Max expressing interest in having one of their stores here in Pine Mountain. It had surprised them to receive the formal letter denying them tax breaks for building their store here."

"So what are they going to do?" I held my breath.

"They don't want any trouble, and are willing to back off. They have several other sites that are more willing to let the store in their town."

I released my breath on a sigh, sinking back in my chair. "That's a relief. Maybe now that stain can be removed from Max's memory." I didn't question why I was fighting so hard to clear his name other than it hurt Jim that people thought his brother was a thief.

"What was on that file?" he asked.

"A bunch of spreadsheets," I said. "I downloaded the file to a thumb drive for you. Maybe the auditors can figure out what it is. Accounting was never my strong suit."

"What are we doing tonight for dinner?" He changed the subject.

"We?" I questioned.

"Sure, we're still trying to get to know the adult us, aren't we?" His chuckle tickled my ear through the telephone line. "We can't do that unless we spend time together."

My heart fluttered in my chest. How long was this going to

take? "Come over when you get off shift," I finally said. "I'll make dinner. It's your turn to cook next time," I challenged.

"Great, I have a few standard dishes I can make. You still like Mexican food, right?"

"Yes, but if one of the things you can make is reservations, that doesn't count," I said with a laugh. "You need to know how to cook."

"I'll have you know I'm a great cook." He paused. "I just don't have a big selection to choose from. Maybe that's something we can work on together. Among other things," his voice dropped to a seductive whisper, causing my heart to flutter. He chuckled again when he heard me gulp. "I'll see you at six. Does that give you enough time when you get off work?" With thoughts of our upcoming dinner crowding my mind, I had trouble concentrating on work for the remainder of the afternoon.

Homemade mac and cheese with Vienna sausages was one of the dinners Mom made when I was growing up. It was simple and fast. I even had all the ingredients at home so I wouldn't have to go shopping after I left work. If memory served, Drake had loved it every time she made it when she and Jim were married. I'd added my own touch by adding green chilies and buttered bread crumbs on top.

The green chilies and sausages scented the air when Drake knocked on my door at six sharp. He'd brought a bottle of my favorite wine with him. I'm not sure wine goes with mac and cheese though.

Without setting down the bottle, he pulled me in for a kiss. His lips moved from mine along my jaw to my ear leaving a trail of goosebumps up my arms. When he released me several minutes later, he sniffed the air. "Something smells good. Whatcha got cooking?"

"One of my standard dishes," I teased. "You'll find out in a few minutes." Slipping his arm around my waist, we headed for the kitchen. I had French bread on top of the stove ready to go under the broiler when I pulled out the casserole dish of mac and cheese.

"Is that your mom's recipe?" Leaning over, he sniffed appreciatively at the bubbling mixture.

"Yes, with a little addition of my own." Handing him the plates and silverware, I let him set the table while I put the garlic bread under the broiler.

Drake waited until we were clearing the table before bringing up the file on my laptop. "How about showing me what you found on that file." A confused frown drew his light colored brows together as he stared at the different screenshots. "I don't think those are the correct account numbers. What is this supposed to prove?"

"I have no idea. That's up to the auditors." I handed over the thumb drive hoping someone could make sense out of them.

"If you don't mind, I'd like to take that in with me." He nodded at the laptop sitting on the table. "Maybe the tech guys can find something else on it. Maybe Max put more on there than that folder."

~~~

We had only been open a few minutes the next morning when Jane rushed through the doors. It was the first time I'd seen her when her hair was tousled, and she didn't have any makeup on. She didn't have Hannah with her either. "I need to talk to you in private," she whispered, leaning over my desk. She was wringing her hands. "You have to help me."

"With what?" If she wanted me to babysit, she should have brought the baby.

"I can't tell you here." She looked around frantically.

"All right, let's go in the back office." I led the way to the combination storeroom and office. Once the door was shut, I looked at her. "We're alone. What is it you need help with?" She was always dramatic, but this was a little over the top.

"Hannah is missing." Tears streamed down her face.

"What do you mean she's missing? Where is she?" In times of stress, I asked the dumbest questions.

"If I knew where she was, she wouldn't be missing," she snapped. "I'm sorry," she lowered her voice. "I need you to help me get her back."

"How can I help you?" Taking her arm, I pushed her into a chair. "If she's missing, you need to call Drake. Are you sure Jim didn't take her to work with him?"

"Why would he do that?" She frowned at me in confusion.

I wasn't sure if it would help to point out the fact that he'd been forced to do that when she spent Thanksgiving night somewhere else. "Um, were you home this morning when he left for work?"

She jumped out of the chair. "Of course I was. What are you suggesting?"

"Sit down, Jane, and tell me what's really going on. Were you up when Jim left?"

"Well, no, but he wouldn't take Hannah to work with him just because I was asleep." She drew a deep breath, letting it out slowly. "I got a call this morning after he left."

"Okay, what did the caller want?" I didn't like the sound of this.

"He said he had Hannah." She started crying, covering her face with her hands.

"Why did you come here? Did you call Jim? Why didn't you call Drake?" I reached for the phone on the counter.

"No." She jumped out of the chair, slapping her hand on top of mine to stop me from picking up the receiver. "He said he'd hurt my baby if I told anyone but you. You have to help me." Tears streaked down her face again.

"Jane, I'm not the police. What do you think I can do? You have to tell Jim. Hannah is his baby, too."

"I know that, but the caller said he'd hurt her if I told anyone." She paced around the confined space.

"How did he get Hannah if you were home? Didn't you hear someone break in?"

"I was very tired after all the company we've had over the holiday. I took a sleeping pill so I'd get a good night's sleep.

He must have been watching for Jim to leave. That's when he took Hannah. She's my baby," she wailed. "You have to help me get her back, Holly. I don't know what to do."

"Jane, I don't know what you expect me to do. I'm not a police officer."

"I know that," she snapped. Her tears dried up quickly with her temper "I just know he said you're the only one I could tell. He wants us to come to Blue Lake. He said he'd meet us at some motel."

"That's twenty miles away."

"I know that. Please, stop asking questions. I don't want anything to happen to my baby. You have to come with me." She kept saying that, but something was wrong with this scenario. When I hesitated, she continued. "If you really loved Hannah, you wouldn't want her to be hurt either." She added guilt to her plea.

I wasn't sure what choice I had. I didn't want anything to happen to Hannah, but I didn't see this ending happily. If this guy was a killer, he wasn't going to let me or Hannah go. "Did he say why he wants me to come? That doesn't make any sense." Why would a killer kidnap Hannah if he was trying to get me? I had to convince her to call Drake. "Jane, we can't go somewhere without telling someone. Don't you think Jim has the right to know Hannah has been kidnapped?"

"No, I mean yes, he has that right, but he'll want to call Drake. Then this guy will hurt my baby. You have to come with me." She was urging me towards the door.

"Where in Blue Lake am I supposed to go?"

"It's a little motel. He gave me the name. Come on, let's go. I want my baby." Her tears had dried up, and she was all business now.

"I need my purse, and I have to tell Linda that I'll be gone for a while." I edged towards my desk. I wasn't sure how I could signal her that something was going on.

"Is everything all right?" Linda came up to my desk as I picked up my purse.

"Um, I have to go out for a little while. Can you handle things here?" I was getting a bad feeling about this. I hoped she was able to pick up on my uncertainty.

"Of course, will you be back before closing?" She looked between Jane and me.

"I think so." I looked at Jane for confirmation. She had her hands clenched together to keep them from shaking. "I have a lunch date with Drake at noon," I stalled. "Can you let him know I might not be back in time?"

"No," Jane snapped. "I mean, you can call him from the car. Besides, I'm sure we'll be back before noon." People in the lobby were beginning to take interest in our little drama. "We need to leave now." She urged me towards the door before I could say anything else.

Outside, I reached in my purse for my phone. "What do you think you're doing?" She grabbed my purse away from me. Her voice held a note of panic.

"I need to call Drake to cancel our lunch." I hoped she'd believed that lie.

"That's not necessary. We'll be back in time."

"How can you be sure of that? If we're dealing with a kidnapper, he isn't just going to let us go." I turned towards the back of the building where my car was parked, but she grabbed my arm.

"We can take my car. It'll be faster. I know where we're going." She pushed me towards her little sports car. "Just get in." She tossed my purse in the back seat.

"Jane, what's really going on? Did someone really kidnap Hannah?"

"Yes, why don't you believe me?" Tears swam in her eyes again.

"You're just acting funny."

"You'd act funny too if your baby had been kidnapped. I want to get her back before something bad happens to her."

"Then why didn't you call Drake? You need to call Jim to let him know. He should know about this."

"I told you, he said he would hurt Hannah if I called anyone but you. Now, just sit there and be quiet. I need to think." For the next few minutes the only sound was the roar of the powerful engine of her sports car.

Please, God. If someone really did kidnap Hannah, please keep her safe. She's so little.

Looking up from my lap, I realized we were going in the wrong direction. "If we're going to Blue Lake, you need to turn around." My heart was doing flip flops now. Whatever was going on, Jane was a part of it. I was certain of that now.

"That's not where we're going," she confirmed my suspicion. "I had to say that, or you wouldn't come with me. I'm following the directions I was given."

"What directions are those? What does the kidnapper want with me?" A strange calm came over me. If Hannah and I were to get out of this unharmed, I needed to keep my head.

"You can ask him when we get where we're going." She turned off the highway onto a forest road. After a mile or so, the pavement turned into gravel until it became nothing more than a dirt track. The low slung car bounced over the potholes in the rutted road. Jane swore softly with each bump. She didn't want her pretty little car ruined.

She finally stopped beside what was little more than a lean-to in the forest. We could hear the cries of a baby as we stepped out of the car. She rushed inside, announcing, "We're here."

"It took you long enough," the man grumbled. I swallowed a gasp before it could escape my mouth. He wasn't alone with Hannah.

CHAPTER SEVENTEEN

Jane hurried across the small enclosure to where Wendell Kramer was holding Hannah. "What did you do to her?" Jane reached out to take Hannah from him.

"Nothing! She's been like this ever since you left. She wants her 'dada.' I tried telling her I'm her dada, but she didn't listen."

"She's a baby, of course she didn't listen." She gave him a look filled with disgust as she rocked back and forth to comfort the crying baby. It was the first time I'd seen her show any real affection for her daughter. Hannah's tears slowed, but didn't stop.

If Jane was to be believed, Hannah had been taken from her bed. The blanket sleeper she was wearing would keep her warm, but not for long. The temperature hovered in the fifties, and the sorry excuse for a cabin had gaping holes in the walls. There was no glass where there should be windows, allowing the wind to whistle through the open spaces.

It was clear Hannah hadn't been kidnapped. Jane was a part of this. This wasn't going to turn out so well. I quietly moved over to the other occupant in the cabin. "Beth Ann? What are you doing here?" Where did she fit in? Why was she here? "What's going on?" I whispered. While Jane and Wendell ignored us I needed to figure out who the players were. "Why are you here?"

"I'm not really sure." She looked puzzled.

"Do you know what's going on? Did he kidnap Hannah?"

Beth Ann shrugged. "I was just told to come out here."

"Why? What do you have to do with them?" She shrugged again, but didn't say anything.

Jane looked at us, aware of the other woman for the first time. "Beth Ann? What are you doing here?" She echoed my question. Turning to look at Wendell, she looked genuinely mystified about Beth Ann's presence.

"Never mind that." Wendell Kramer snapped. He stepped in front of me, shooting daggers at me. "I want our money. Where did you put it?" His voice was a snarl.

I stepped away from his fury. "What are you talking about? I don't have your money."

"Well, someone took it."

"Why do you think I had anything to do with that?" I kept an eye on Jane while keeping track of Wendell as he paced around the small enclosure. Beth Ann moved away from me, leaning against the wall crossing her arms over her ample chest. If she wasn't careful, it would collapse under her weight.

"Max said he had evidence of what we'd done. You're the only person he saw before I…" His voice trailed off.

"Before you killed him?" I raged. "Is that what you were trying to say?" I would have rushed at him ready to scratch his eyes out, but his arm flashed out, backhanding me across the face. I stumbled backwards, landing on my backside on the dirt floor. Jane screamed, causing Hannah to start crying again.

"Why did you do that?" Jane grabbed at his arm, trying to pull him away from me. "We need her to tell us where our money is." Beth Ann didn't move. A small smile lifted the corners of her lips.

"If she doesn't have it, where is it?" He shook off her grasp. He turned to glare at Beth Ann, but he quickly dropped his gaze to the dirt floor. She hadn't moved, but he was oddly intimidated by her. "She has to know where he put it," he said, talking to the floor. "Max said we'd never get our hands on it."

Those screenshots Max left on my laptop had to have something to do with where the money is. A few things were beginning to fall into place. Wendell worked in the IT department. He had access to Max's email account, along with anything on the server.

With Max's passcodes he was able to get into the bank accounts. He would know how to manipulate the information to make it look like Max had transferred the money. I hoped

Drake's people could find it and us before this guy lost all control. Had I been wrong about Jack Johnston? Maybe he didn't have anything to do with Dynamic Corporation wanting to build a store in Pine Mountain. Drake never said Johnston was involved with that. Maybe I'd been wrong.

"I told you we should have left town as soon as Max figured out what we were doing." He frowned at Jane. "But no, you still wanted to get your pound of flesh from your husband."

"I wanted something out of this marriage. You aren't the one who had to suffer with an old man groping you. I thought he'd add my name to the ranch and store so I could get my share in a divorce. But no, everything he has is tied up in a stupid trust." She released a frustrated breath. She'd been using Jim all along. She was only after his money.

"You said no one would ever be able to figure out your game" she accused. "You said you were smarter than everyone in this hick town. That didn't turn out so well, did it? I don't know why I ever thought you could get away with this."

"Don't try to put the blame all on me," he snapped. "This is as much your fault as it is mine." He ran his fingers through his hair in frustration. "Can't you shut the kid up?" he shouted, making Hannah cry harder. The crying baby was beginning to wear on their nerves. I needed to get her away from Jane before they both lost it.

"That's no way to talk about your baby." She sniffled, blinking her eyes rapidly. My mouth dropped open. What was she saying? I stared at them from my place on the floor. Was this man, this killer, Hannah's biological father? I stared at Hannah trying to pick out features from Jim.

Wendell went over to Jane, giving her and Hannah a hug. "I'm sorry. You know I didn't mean that, but I can't think straight with her crying all the time. We have to make her tell us where our money is. Without it, we can't go anywhere."

I had no idea where the money was. Drake said the money

hadn't been transferred to the account it had been intended for. If he didn't find us soon, this wasn't going to turn out well for me. They had already said enough to hang themselves. I didn't believe they were naïve enough to think I wouldn't tell everything once I was found. My heart was in my throat at what this meant. They weren't planning on letting me go.

I didn't know how I was going to get out alive. I wouldn't leave without Hannah, and I wouldn't let them take her. I needed to stall for time. As long as they were arguing, there was the chance that Drake would find us. I had to keep them talking. "How did you think you were going to get away with this?"

"Max was a con man, plain and simple. I don't know what Jim was thinking when he put him in charge of the town's money. When Jim gave that job to his no-count brother, I knew what I could do. I'd already been syphoning money out of the accounts. I didn't think anyone would notice."

"But Max did notice," I said.

"Not right away." He shook his head. "When he did, I conned the con man." He chuckled, bragging about his accomplishments. "I told him it was just a game. I even conned him into playing along. We would see who could get away with taking the most money without getting caught. He thought we were playing with phony accounts. But I was playing for real." He drew a shaky breath.

"When he realized what I was doing, he threatened to turn me in. But I had outsmarted him. He was the one that would go to jail. You see, all along I made it look like Max was the one taking the money." He was proud of what he'd done. "When he disappeared, I thought we were done for. But it worked against him instead. Everyone knew his reputation. They believed he was the one that took the money." He chuckled again.

"If you're really that smart, why did you turn to stealing? Why not get a good job?" Struggling to my feet, I wiped at the thin trickle of blood from the cut on my lip. I didn't care if he hit me again as long as he stayed away from Hannah. They seemed to have forgotten about Beth Ann. It didn't appear that she was interested in getting away either.

"Do you know how hard it is to get ahead in a small town?" he asked. "Unless you know someone, you're going to be stuck in some go nowhere job for the rest of your life." He got right in my face, yelling at me. "A college education no longer guarantees a good paying job. How am I supposed to support my family on what I make?"

"You can't expect to earn top dollar right out of college," I tried to reason with him. "You could have gotten a job and worked your way up." He'd spend the rest of his life in prison now. But only if Drake found us in time. The thought was depressing.

"Sure, that easy for you to say," he sneered. "You got a job because Jim's your stepfather." He seemed to forget that Jim hadn't been that for a long time. "What about the little guy who doesn't have someone pulling strings for him?" he continued to rail. "Until someone higher up the ladder dies or quits, I'm stuck doing the same menial job day after day."

I knew I had gotten my job because of my relationship with Jim. But I didn't want to think there was someone with the same qualifications that got passed over because of it. Linda didn't want the job. Was there someone else who did? I gave a mental shrug. I couldn't think about that now. I needed to concentrate on getting Hannah and me away from them.

"So why did you come to a small town? Why not live in a big city where more jobs are available and you could work your way up?"

"Because Jane and Hannah are here. Are you really that stupid? I needed to be close to them." Hannah's cries had turned into hiccups, but at his shout she started crying again. He shot Jane a warning look. "Besides, big-paying jobs aren't any easier to find there than they are here. It all boils down to who you know, not what you know. I don't know anyone. My folks don't have any clout. How am I supposed to get ahead without someone to help me?" He had the same entitled attitude of so many young people. They wanted everything handed to them.

"Stop arguing with her, and make her tell us where the money is." Jane stepped in front of him. "She's stalling for time." Hannah had worn herself out, and was almost asleep on Jane's shoulder. Her breathing shuddered with each breath.

"Why do you think I know where the money is? I had nothing to do with this." I kept praying that Linda had called Drake. We didn't have a lunch date, and he would know something was wrong. I had to keep them talking long enough for him to find us. I wasn't sure the GPS on my phone still worked in the forest though.

"Max gave you something when he went to see you. What was it? You need to give it to me right now." Wendell's question brought me back to the present.

I shook my head. "He didn't give me anything."

"He had to. He said he left evidence of what I'd done. You're the only one he saw after he disappeared."

"How do you know that? Were you following him?"

"Because I'm smarter than he was," he boasted. "I knew he wouldn't leave town without trying to clear his name. I figured he'd turn to one of his nephews. I wasn't far wrong. He went to his niece instead. I caught him leaving your place."

"Well, he didn't give me anything that night. Maybe he left it wherever his was hiding."

He shook his head. "It's not here." He looked around the small enclosure. "If he didn't give you anything, who took our money?" The question wasn't so much for me as it was for himself.

"Did you break into my house?"

"Yeah, and I owe you one for this." He lifted his pant leg revealing a large bruise where I'd hit him with the broom stick. "It's payback time now." He raised his hand to hit me again, but Jane grabbed his arm to stop him.

"Stick with the program so we can get out of here. I'm

about to freeze." She had on a light-weight sweater and fashion jeans that fit like a second skin, neither of which was meant to keep her warm.

"Maybe Fred moved it," I said. "He caught on to what you were doing. That's why he was so nervous when I went to see him. Isn't that why you killed him?" Beth Ann made no attempt to escape even though it appeared they had forgotten about her. I still didn't understand why she was there.

"No, he was helping us. He was my half-brother." He looked close to tears now.

"You killed your own brother?" I gasped. "How could you do that?" This was getting worse with everything he said.

"*Half*-brother," he said, stressing the half.

"Well, I have several of those, and I've never killed one of them."

"It wasn't like that. It was an accident. It was your fault. If you hadn't been poking around, asking him questions, he wouldn't have panicked. He wanted me to give the money back. When I wouldn't do that, he said he'd tell. I couldn't let him do that. I had to protect my family."

"What family? Jane is married to Jim, and Hannah is his daughter."

"No, she's my daughter, and Jane loves me." He turned to Jane. "Tell her," he demanded.

"Of course I love you." He didn't notice that she didn't say Hannah was his daughter.

"Then why did you marry Jim?" I asked. I kept stalling. As long as they were talking, there was still the chance Drake would find us.

"Duh, he had money." She made it sound like a no brainer. "He said I would never want for anything. I didn't count on living in some back-water town, and being saddled with a baby."

"Saddled with a baby?" Wendell sounded shocked at that. "I thought you loved our baby." His face was getting red with anger.

"Of course I love her. I just didn't expect to have one so soon. I thought we'd be together before that happened." She moved up close to him, trying to soothe his hurt feelings.

"It doesn't matter when it happened. I love her. She's my daughter." I couldn't see any resemblance to him. His hair was dark brown; Hannah's was the same shade of sandy brown as Jim's.

"Maybe the bank found where you transferred the money, and got it back," I suggested, hoping to distract them.

"I'm not that stupid," he snapped. "It was in a numbered account in the Caymans. I had a passcode on the account. Without that, no one could touch the account, and I'm the only one that knows it." Jane jerked around to glare at him. Something told me that even she didn't know it. That didn't sit well with her either.

"Are you behind that big store coming to town, too?" I asked. As long as he was willing to tell me all of his misdeeds, I figured I'd check that one out as well. I didn't want to accuse Jack Johnston of something he hadn't done.

"Hell no," he exclaimed. "How would that store benefit me?" Of course, he didn't care about anything that wasn't a benefit to him. It was stupid of me to think otherwise.

"So there are two crooks on the town payroll." It wasn't a question.

"I'm not a crook," he shouted, rousing Hannah out of her light sleep causing her to cry again. Jane shushed her when he turned to glare at her.

"No?" I lifted an eyebrow at him. "What do you call murder?"

"I told you I had to do that. I was protecting my family. It isn't murder if you're protecting someone."

"That isn't exactly how that works. There's still the fact that you embezzled the town's money. That's illegal, and you can't explain it away."

"The town has insurance, so does the bank," he scoffed. "The insurance company would replace the money. No one was supposed to get hurt."

"That's insurance fraud. The list of your crimes is getting longer."

"No, I'm not a criminal." He stormed at me, shoving me against the wall. To everyone's surprise the rickety wall gave way under the sudden pressure, and I found myself on the ground outside.

Wendell stepped over the broken boards, looking down at me. "Are you all right?" He was as shocked as I was by what had happened.

The breath had been knocked out of my lungs, and I took several gasping breath. "What do you think?" I asked when I could talk again. I moved slowly, assessing whether anything was broken. The rotten boards had easily given way, slowing down my momentum as I fell. There were scrapes on both palms, and it hurt to move my wrist, but I considered myself lucky. It could have been worse.

He reached at his hand to help me up, but I didn't want his help. Cradling my sore arm against my ribs, I struggled to my feet for the second time. They weren't career criminals, just greedy and lazy. That didn't mean they weren't going to go to prison. Two men were dead because of them. Before that could happen though, I had to get away. The gaping hole in the wall was the ideal escape route, but I wasn't leaving without Hannah. I wasn't sure how I was going to accomplish that.

"Will you get on with this," Jane snapped. "I don't want to stay in this hovel all night. It's getting even colder in here since she knocked that wall down."

"Gee, I'm sorry about that," I said sarcastically. "I didn't mean to inconvenience you. Oh, wait a minute. I didn't do that. Your boyfriend pushed me hard enough to knock it down." I held up my arm to show where my wrist was beginning to swell. "I don't particularly want to stay here overnight either. How about we go back to town? I'm sure by now Jim has figured out Hannah is missing. You know he'll call Drake right away."

"I took care of that little problem," she said smugly. "I left him a note that I went to be with my mother. She's getting old and wanted to spend more time with Hannah. He won't miss either of us for several days."

My hopes plummeted. They'd thought of almost everything. *Lord Jesus, please help me find a way out of this. Hannah deserves to have a good life with parents that love her, not killers and crooks*

"If you'll tell us where you moved the money, we'll let you go," Wendell said. "We don't want to hurt you."

They must think I'm pretty stupid if they expect me to believe that lie. I know who they are. To buy time, I decided to go along with the assumption that they would let me go.

"I don't know where the money is, but..." I held up my hand when he started to interrupt me. "Someone put a file on my laptop."

Excited, both Jane and Wendell got closer to me. "What's on it? It probably tells where our money is." Out of the corner of my eye, I noticed that Beth Ann straightened away from the wall anticipating my answer.

"Well, I wasn't sure if Max put it there or if the person who broke into my house did. I knew whoever stole all that money was smart enough to put a virus on my computer if they thought Max had e-mailed something to me. I didn't want to lose all of my files." I played up to his ego.

"Yes, that is something I would do. But I didn't have the chance. Where is your laptop?" He was almost salivating at the thought of being this close to the money.

"It's at work," I shrugged. "Jane hustled me out of the library so fast I barely had time to grab my purse. Maybe we can go back there and get it now."

Wendell had to think about that for several minutes as he paced around. He finally shook his head. "We'll go back there when it's dark. You have keys to the library, so we can go in then." Right now that was my best hope. There is an alarm on all the doors. Putting in the incorrect code would set off a silent alarm.

It was going to be a long wait. It wasn't even noon yet.

"Okay, enough chit chat, let's cut to the chase." We had all forgotten about Beth Ann until she spoke up for the first time. "You're not going anywhere. I want to know where my money is." Pulling a small gun out of the big bag she carried, she pointed it me. She wasn't a hostage, she was part of this.

"It's not your money," Wendell argued. "It's mine."

She gave a humorless laugh. "If you want to be technical, it belongs to the good people of Pine Mountain. I still can't believe the geeky little guy in college won the heart of the captain of the cheerleading team. Go figure."

That was the connection between them, I thought. *They went to college together.* I didn't know how Jim got tangled up with them.

Beth Ann swept the gun around the room. "But then you had the balls to actually steal money from the town." She snickered.

"I did it because I'm smart."

"No, you did it because you needed money to keep that little gold digger."

"I'm not a gold digger. I love Wendell."

"Of course you do, Honey, you just love money more, or you wouldn't have married a man old enough to be your father. You thought you could take him to the cleaners. But you didn't count on that little bundle of joy." This time she pointed the gun at Hannah.

Wendell and I both moved in front of Jane. If Beth Ann was going to shoot someone, it wouldn't be Hannah. "Oh, don't worry. She's not the one I'm going to shoot." She raised the gun, pointing it at Jane's head.

Giving a squeal, Jane jumped, nearly dropping the baby. I grabbed her in time to keep that from happening. She relinquished her without an argument. Instead, she shrunk down behind Wendell.

Beth Ann gave her a disgusted look. "All you care about is your own skin."

"That's not true," Wendell defended Jane against the verbal attack. "She loves me."

"Right, that's why she's letting you shield her from harm."

"Isn't a man supposed to protect those he loves? I'd do anything for Jane and Hannah."

She shook her head in disgust. "I guess you proved that when you murdered your own brother." He started to argue, but thought better of it when she raised the gun to his head.

While they argued, I took baby steps towards the broken-down wall. If I could make it outside, I had a chance of running into the forest.

"Fred only went along with this because he was in love with you," he whimpered instead. "But you played both him and Max for fools. You were only interested in the money."

My mouth dropped open. I hadn't seen that coming. I managed not to say anything though as I got a little closer to the broken wall.

"You were sleeping with Max and Fred?" Jane stood up so she could stare at Beth Ann.

"Fred was a little young and inexperienced for me," she chuckled. "I was sleeping with Max. He was good-looking, and he liked buying me nice things. Everything was going fine until this idiot got greedy."

I was a few steps away from freedom when she swung around, pointing the gun at me. "I'm running out of patience, Holly. Tell me where my money is."

"I don't know where the money is. Why do you even think I do?"

"Because you are the last one to see my darling Max before lover-boy here shot him. Did you know he couldn't stop singing your praises?" she sneered. "I got so tired of hearing how wonderful you are I was ready to shoot him myself. He thought you were smart, and beautiful." It was like she was jealous of me.

She shook her head. "He didn't realize until it was too late that I'm smarter than all of you put together."

"That's what he meant when he said this was his fault. He said he was sorry for everything because he realized you weren't the woman he thought you were." I glared at Beth Ann.

"I am smart," Wendell said. "I had it all planned out. All I needed was a few more days, and we would have been gone." He wasn't bragging anymore. He was lamenting the fact that Max had figured out his scheme.

"You couldn't outsmart Max though, could you?" Beth Ann taunted. "He figured out what you were doing, and did something with the money before you could get away. Well, I'm smarter than both of you put together. The money belongs to me now."

"No, it's mine, not yours." They were like two children arguing over a toy. He lunged at her. The loud gun shot was deafening. Wendell gasped as he crumpled to the ground. Jane screamed, dropping down beside him. Startled out of her semi-sleep, Hannah began crying. I took another step towards the broken wall, hoping to make good our escape.

"Not so fast." Beth Ann turned away from the two people on the floor. She stepped between me and the broken wall. There was no way for me to escape with Hannah now. "I'm done asking nicely. I want that money. Just tell me what was on that file, and I'll leave you here alive." The gun was pointed at my head.

"I don't know what is on that file. Honest. If you kill me, you'll never know either. If you are so smart, why don't you know where the money is?"

"It never made it to Wendell's account. Max did something. He said he wasn't going to let them get away with this. Tell me what was on that file Max left for you?"

"I don't know."

"You bitch. You killed him. How could you do that?" Beth Ann had forgotten about Jane until she leaped up from the floor. Her fingers were curled into claws. The red nail polish looked like blood dripping from her fingertips. But maybe that's what it was. She had been pressing her hands to the gaping wound on Wendell's chest.

Beth Ann whirled around in time to catch Jane across the face with the gun, sending her sprawling. She was unconscious, but at least she was alive. Hannah was hysterical from the noise of the gun shot.

Looking back at me, Beth Ann smiled. "With that dirty business taken care of, I'll ask you one last time. What was on that file? It will tell me where my money is." She raised the gun, pointing it at my head again.

"Drop the gun, Beth Ann, or I'll drop you." Drake appeared out of nowhere. His gun was pointed at her.

She looked over her shoulder at him, judging her chances of talking him out of this situation. "Suicide by cop is better than the next twenty years in jail. You'll have my blood on your hands. Can you live with that?"

"It doesn't have to be that way. Just put down the gun." Drake gave a slight nod as she looked over her shoulder at him. Hoping I understood his signal correctly, I sank down to the ground, pressing my hand over Hannah's ear.

"Sure it does." She gave a sad smile, swinging her arm around. The explosion from Drake's gun was loud in the still air. Beth Ann dropped like she was in a slow motion movie.

Suddenly there were cops everywhere. Kicking the gun out of Beth Ann's still hand, Drake knelt down beside me. Wrapping us in his arms, he rocked back and forth. "Thank you, God," I whispered against Drake's neck. I wasn't sure how he found us, but I was thankful that he had.

CHAPTER EIGHTEEN

Jane moaned from her position on the dirt floor. The cut on her face where Beth Ann hit her was still bleeding. "What happened?" She blinked her eyes, trying to bring things into focus. Seeing Drake, she struggled to get up. "Oh, thank God you're here. I thought we were all going to be killed." She looked at Beth Ann lying beside Wendell's still body. "She was crazed, they both were. Thank you for saving us." She moved towards Drake.

"Just stay where you are, Jane, until we get this sorted out." He stood up, stepping in front of her. "Are you all right, Holly?" He looked down at me, his eyes dark with emotion.

"I will be now." I was still sitting on the cold ground, and was beginning to shiver.

"Drake, I need to see if Hannah's all right. She's traumatized by this whole experience. She needs her mother." Her voice was pleading, and she tried to stand up again.

"I said to stay where you are." His voice was commanding, freezing her in mid-stance.

"Why are you treating me like this? Can't you see I've been hurt? I need a doctor. I haven't done anything wrong. I'm a victim, too."

"That's to be determined. Right now, you aren't going anywhere."

"You can't stop me from taking care of my daughter," she said defiantly.

"Holly will make sure she's all right." He motioned to Officer Babcock. "Put her in the back of your car for now."

"Are you arresting me?" Jane's voice rose to a shriek. "I haven't done anything wrong."

"Seriously, Jane?" I stared at her dumbfounded. "I was right here. I heard it all." I struggled to my feet with Hannah in my arms. My injured wrist throbbed with every movement.

"I had to say those things. I was protecting my daughter.

He threatened me."

Wendell was dead so he couldn't defend himself. But there wasn't much he could have said. He had killed two people.

Drake jerked his head towards the patrol cars that had pulled up beside the rickety cabin. She struggled against Babcock's efforts to lead her to the waiting vehicle. "No, I haven't done anything wrong." She tried to jerk away from him. "I want my daughter. You can't take her away from me. I have rights."

"You can tell your side of things in due time. Right now, you're going to be sitting in the back of that car." His voice was gravelly with emotions held in check. She continued to struggle against the officer until the car door slammed on her insults.

Turning back to me, he pulled me into his arms. His embrace was so tight, I could barely draw a breath, but I didn't care. We were safe. That's all that mattered at the moment. "You took ten years off my life today. Do you feel up to telling me what happened here?" The crime scene unit showed up before I could answer. He stepped away from me to give them directions.

I didn't know how long we'd been out there. It felt like days. If the warm, wet spot on my blouse was any indication, it had been a long time since anyone had thought to change Hannah's diaper. At least Jane had brought the diaper bag.

"Can I change her diaper while I talk?" My hands were shaking and my legs felt like rubber as the adrenaline drained from my blood stream. I didn't know how policemen and soldiers lived with this sort of thing.

Drake's SUV was just out of sight in the trees. Taking us there, he kept his arm around my waist like he was afraid to let me go for fear I'd disappear.

"How did you find us?" I finally managed to ask. Drake turned the car on, and it only took a few minutes for the heater to warm up the interior. Once she was warm and dry, Hannah fell asleep again. I had crackers in my purse for her when she

NEVER CON A CON MAN

woke up. Jane hadn't thought to pack any food for her again.

"Linda called minutes after you left with Jane. She said you asked her to call and cancel our lunch date, which we didn't have." He gave me a small smile. "That was quick thinking. She said you never left the library during open hours unless it was an emergency." I had moved from the back seat to sit in the circle of his arms.

"Linda said Jane didn't have Hannah with her, so I called Dad to check on her. That was the first he knew about any of this. Jane's phone was turned off. I couldn't reach you on your cell phone either."

"Jane took my purse away from me when I tried to call you. It's in the back seat of her car."

"Dad found the note she'd left him when he went out to the ranch." He shook his head in disbelief. "She's not going to be able to lie her way out of this."

"How did you find the shack? Jane drove several miles on that dirt track."

"Tracking the GSP on your phone only worked so far. Once you went into the forest, the signal was lost. I remembered someone telling me Bill knows the forest like the back of his hand." He gave me a weary smile. "This is the shack we played in when we were kids."

He looked over his shoulder at the ramshackle building. "It's in worse shape than it had been then. I can't believe she let him take Hannah to such a place. What happened to that wall?

As I told him about Wendell pushing me through the wall, his fingers tightened on mine. "Just a sprain," I said. "It feels better already. I might have a few broken fingers if you don't relax." I tried to wiggle loose.

"Sorry," he muttered. Relaxing his grip, he didn't let go of my hand.

Bill was with his dad at the police station when we finally got back to town. Drake hadn't placed Jane under arrest yet, and she rushed at Jim with her arms out. "Darling, I was so afraid. They won't let me hold Hannah. Tell Drake that I'm a victim, too. He won't even let me see a doctor."

He gripped her shoulders, pushing her away, and moved to take Hannah who had started fussing again when she saw her daddy. Without a word to Jane, he headed for the door. Bill followed him out, but not before Drake clasped his shoulder. He couldn't form the words thanking him for his help. Giving a nod of understanding, Bill followed Jim outside.

"Damn it, Jim," Jane cursed, stomping her foot in frustration. She whirled around on Drake. "Why won't you let me go home? I haven't done anything wrong." She was still trying to bluff her way through this.

"No?" Drake relaxed casually on the corner of the desk. "What do you call embezzlement, murder and kidnapping?"

Her face blanched, and she sat down before she collapsed when her legs wouldn't hold her up any longer.

"He made me do those things. He was obsessed with me. He's been stalking me for years. I haven't done anything wrong," she said weakly. There was no conviction in her voice.

"You didn't take Holly out there?" His tone was mild, but there was ice in his eyes now.

"I had to, he had my baby." She buried her face in her hands, crying like her heart was broken. She deserved the academy award for this performance. "He made me bring her out there. You don't understand what it's like to see your baby in the hands of someone like him."

"Aren't you forgetting something, Jane?" I interrupted her little scene.

"What's that?" I would have believed the innocence in her beautifully made up eyes if I hadn't been in that cabin with them.

"I was there, Jane. I heard everything the three of you said."

"You believed that?" She gave a small laugh. "I had to play along or he would have hurt Hannah. She's such a sweet baby. I couldn't let anything happen to her." Tears shimmered in her eyes.

For a half second I almost believed her. I shook my head. "You're good, but not that good. You wanted that money as much as Wendell and Beth Ann did. It was your ticket out of here."

"No, I just said all that so he wouldn't hurt Hannah. You have to believe me."

"That's enough, Jane." Taking her arm in a rough grip, Drake lifted her out of the chair. Placing her in a small room, he left her there to consider what his next move might be.

Once we were alone, he sat down, pulling me onto his lap, burying his face in my hair. He took several unsteady breaths before allowing me to sit in the chair beside him.

"Without Bill's help, we'd still be searching for you. I couldn't even remember where that stupid cabin was." He drew a shaky breath. "There's no telling what they would have done. Why did you go with her?"

"She said Hannah had been kidnapped."

"So why didn't she call me?"

"Supposedly the kidnapper called her and said I was the only one she could tell."

"Why? What were you supposed to do?" A frown drew his brows into a straight line over troubled eyes.

"They wanted the money Wendell had embezzled. Somehow Max had managed to stop them from taking it. He hid it somewhere. That must be what's on that file he put on my laptop."

He nodded his head. "The techs found it along with another file Max placed in with your documents. It explains a whole lot." He shook his head. "He fell for Beth Ann, but she was using him the same way Jane used Dad. He didn't realize what she was doing until it was almost too late."

Drawing a shaky breath, he shook his head. "Max was smarter than they expected. They also thought because of his past they could manipulate him. I don't understand everything he did, but once he caught on to their game, he turned the tables on them. That saying 'Never kid a kidder,' goes double for a con man." He sighed. "Even after Kramer killed him, Max managed to win the con. The money is back in the town's accounts."

"Thank God," I sighed, snuggling as close as our two chairs allowed. I could stay there forever. "Max said this was his last con," I said sadly. "I guess it really was." For several minutes we were silent. Max died because they felt they were entitled to take what they wanted.

"I know who was behind the deal with the store," I finally broke the silence.

When he nodded his head that stray lock of hair fell over his eyes. I reached up, running my fingers through the silly strands. He placed a kiss in my palm, like he had in the past. "Jack Johnston is already out of a job," he stated.

My mouth dropped open. "You knew about that? How?"

"I kept telling you to let me handle it. You gave me the evidence that I needed to keep looking. Our tech guys found the emails. They were all on that file Max left you. It was supposed to look like they came from Max's computer when they really came from Johnston's." He leaned back in the chair, drawing a deep breath. "He wanted to get back at Dad for giving Max the job he wanted. He had a job lined up with Dynamic Corporation once the store opened here."

"So he's out of his job here and doesn't have one with Dynamic either." I shook my head.

"I don't know what Dynamic will do," Drake admitted. "They just might welcome him with open arms. They seem to like things a little on the shady side. Did Wendell say why he killed Fred?" He got us back on track.

Giving my account of all that happened in the few hours I'd been in that small shack took almost as long as I'd been there. I still couldn't believe Wendell would kill his own brother.

Wendell was smart, but he wasn't willing to work for what he wanted. It was easier to steal. Or so he thought. He paid the ultimate price for his greed.

"Now that we have all this taken care of, maybe we can get on with this getting to know the adult us," I teased.

"Hmmm, that sounds like a good idea. Or," he paused. "What would you think if we skipped that part, and got right to the formal proposal?" He pulled a small velvet box out of his pocket. "I've been carrying this around for more than a week. I almost waited too long." A shudder shook him before he pulled me close, his lips claiming mine. It took several minutes to convince him I was fine. Lifting his head, he rested his forehead against mine. "This isn't the way I'd planned it, but I don't want to waste any more time. Holly Foster, will you do me the honor of becoming my wife?" He didn't get down on one knee, but I didn't mind. Sitting in his lap worked for me. The ring was perfect, just like the man. I gave him my answer with a kiss.

~~~

"I made a lot of mistakes as a mayor and as a man," Jim admitted. We were all gathered at the ranch later that day. He looked down as his daughter sleeping peacefully in his arms. He was afraid to put her in her crib for fear she would disappear again. "I will always be grateful to Jane for this one, but I let her youth and beauty blind me to her true nature. Unfortunately, when she realized they wouldn't be able to get my money, they went looking for another way to get some."

He drew a deep breath letting it out slowly. "I'm going to resign as mayor and concentrate on what's most important." Again he looked down at Hannah.

"Max made a lot of mistakes in his life, but in the end he was a good man. It's too bad he had to pay with his life for the mistake of trusting the wrong woman. I can't believe how Beth Ann had everyone fooled all these years."

"Max proved one thing," Drake said, a sad smile tilting the corners of his mouth.

"What's that?"

"You should never con a con man. Even after he was gone,

Max managed to win the con."

"I still don't understand why Max came to me. We weren't very close."

"Because of that fact, he was counting on them not expecting you to have the evidence he'd collected. Those last few days he was under a lot of stress. He'd been betrayed by the woman he loved, and by his friend. He knew what this was going to do to Dad when he found out about Jane and Wendell." Drake looked over at Jim with sorrow in his eyes.

"Don't worry about me, son. I'm going to be fine."

When Drake formally arrested Jane, her shrieks could be heard throughout the courthouse. She continued to claim she was innocent of any wrongdoing. Although she hadn't taken part in the murder of Max or Fred, she was a part of the crime that led up to their murders. That made her an accessory. She had been part of the embezzlement and kidnapping. I wasn't sure if her claim that I had gone with her of my own freewill would hold up with a jury.

Whatever happened, she wouldn't see Hannah for a long time. Jim made sure of that. Unbeknownst to anyone, he had filed for divorce the day after Thanksgiving. Divorce was hard on children, but Hannah was young enough she wouldn't remember any of this.

"With Jane going to prison, do you think your folks will get back together?" I asked. Drake and I were in my living room later that week.

He chuckled. "Can you really see Mom being happy in Pine Mountain after all these years living in Phoenix?" He shook his head. "No, they're better off as friends. Maybe Dad will eventually find someone to spend the rest of his life with, but it won't be Mom."

Maybe he'd finally notice how much Linda loves him, I thought. But for now, there was a lot of healing to be done. "Does that upset you?" I finally asked.

"Most kids of divorce want their parents to get back together, and I was no different when I was little. But God had other plans. If Mom and Dad had stayed married, Dad never would have met your mom, and I wouldn't have met you. God's plans for us are always better than our plans."

He pulled me into his arms, his lips claiming mine. I said a prayer of thanks that God had been watching over us all this time, and His plans are perfect.

ACKNOWLEDGEMENTS

I thank God for the many wonderful gifts He has given me in this life. Among them are my wonderful family. He has answered my prayers, allowing me to tell my stories and publish my books. I am so blessed.

My thanks and gratitude also goes to Gerry Beamon, Sandy Roedl, and KaTie Jackson for their suggestions, editing and encouragement. I can't forget about all the information retired Phoenix Police Detective Ken Shriner has given me on police procedure. Thanks for your patience, Ken, and for answering my many questions about law enforcement. I apologize for taking literary license with police procedure in an effort to move the story forward.

OTHER BOOKS BY SUZANNE FLOYD

Revenge Served Cold
Rosie's Revenge
A Game of Cat and Mouse
Man on the Run
Trapped in a Whirlwind
Smoke & Mirrors
Plenty of Guilt
Lost Memories
Something Shady
Rosie's Secret
Killer Instincts
Never Con A Con Man
The Games People Play
Family Secrets
Picture That
Trading Places
Chasing His Shadow
Rosie's Legacy

Dear Reader:

Thank you for reading my book. I hope you enjoyed reading it as much as I enjoyed writing it. If you enjoyed Never Con a Con Man, I would appreciate it if you would tell your friends and relatives and/or write a review on Amazon.

Follow me on Facebook at Suzanne Floyd Author, or check out my website at SuzanneFloyd.com.

Thank you,
Suzanne Floyd

P.S. If you find any errors, please let me know at: Suzanne.sfloyd@gmail.com. Before publishing, many people have read this book, but our minds can play tricks on us by supplying words that aren't there and correcting typos.

Thanks again for reading my book.

ABOUT THE AUTHOR

Suzanne is an internationally known author. She was born in Iowa, and moved to Arizona with her family when she was nine years old. She still lives in Phoenix with her husband, Paul. They have two wonderful daughters, two great sons-in-law and five of the best grandchildren around. Of course, she is just a little prejudiced.

Growing up and traveling with her parents, she entertained herself by making up stories. As an adult she tried writing, but family came first. After retiring in 2008, she decided it was her time. She still enjoys making up stories, and thanks to the internet she's able to put them online for others to enjoy.

When Suzanne isn't writing, she and her husband enjoy traveling around on their 2010 Honda Goldwing trike. She's always looking for new places to write about. There's always a new mystery and a romance lurking out there to capture her attention.

Made in the USA
Columbia, SC
26 January 2022